For my mom

Out of her window, Peggy watched as the snow began to fall on the avenue below. The streetlamps were lit, and the snowflakes danced in the yellow glow. She pulled her soft brown and red afghan tighter over her shoulders and tucked her feet in under the blanket. The window seat in her tiny room was her favourite place to be alone. She could hear the other girls in the boarding house giggling and scurrying around. There was a crash and then a loud gasp, followed by peals of laughter that Peggy knew could only be from Mary.

"Peg!! Come on!!" Mary had poked her curly, blonde head around the door. "It's snowing! Audrey and Kate and I are going out to catch the flakes!"

Mary was a golden child, in the truest sense of the word. Her laugh was infectious, she was witty and impetuous, but only insofar as she was endearing, not a bit reckless. She had close-cropped blonde curls that would not stay in place no matter how much Aqua Net was lacquered to it, nor how many bobby pins were strategically placed, and thus, Mary gave up and "let it live". She had lively blue eyes, ruddy cheeks, with no need for blush, full lips quick to smile, and an aquiline nose. She wore becoming clothes in her colours, which flattered her charming little figure. She was in the city attending the Women's College. Her parents were hoping that she would obtain her degree and find a nice lawyer to wed. Mary was keen on the plan but insisted that she "might as well have a blast" in the meantime. Now, her bright eyes danced, as she stood in the doorway of Peggy's room. Her warm black boots gave way to bright red tights, beneath her thick woolen skirt and tweed jacket. She wore blue mittens, the same shade as her eyes, and the same shade as the toque pulled low over her forehead. The whole effect was just as entrancing as Mary herself.

"You girls go on. I am nursing a cold and Mr. Reynolds would flip out if I caught a chill and couldn't make it to work tomorrow."

Peggy picked up the teacup from the little wooden table next to her as if to emphasize her point. She took a sip of the now lukewarm tea and looked beseechingly over the rim at her friend. Mary shrugged and banged the door closed behind her.

"No dice, girls! Peg's dullsville tonight. Let's go!!"

Peggy slumped back against her stack of cushions and looked back out the window. This was going to be her first winter away from home, and the thought filled her with an odd sensation. It was both a longing for Mama and Dad, a longing to go home and feel safe, and a bubbling excitement at what was ahead of her. In the spring, she had earned her bachelor's and had spent the summer applying for any job she could get her elegant hands on, to earn enough to get herself to the city. She scrimped and saved and went two seasons without a good haircut. Her mother tsked when they drove into town and Peggy refused to buy a new summer hat at JC Penney.

"Mama, last year's hat will do just fine, thank you. I need the money for room and board come Fall."

"Oh, darling! Mrs. Brennan exclaimed in genuine horror that her youngest daughter would be seen around town and in Church in last year's hat. But you must have a new hat! It is really a much better investment in your future than room and board to go gallivanting off to the city, like some sort of... well, let's just say that no Brennan has ever lived on her own!!"

Mrs. Brennan was a traditional woman and had married her husband at the ripe old age of 19 and believed herself to be happy for it. Peggy did not see this as so. How could a woman be happy, living in a big house, away from friends and family, tending to five children, at one point five under the age of five, and all that that entailed? Mrs. Brennan scrubbed and waxed her floors, did the washing, cooking, laundry, dusting, canning, sewing, knitting, gardening, and chased after her children. Peggy saw this as a woman gone mad, rather than a woman who 'had it all'. Mr. Brennan left at seven o'clock each morning, with a quick peck on the cheek from his wife, to take the train into town, where he spent the day in his office, making important decisions, and lunching with entertaining people, and being a part of the world. Peggy thought her father's life was splendid. He had a secretary, and an expense account and folks took him seriously. At home, Peggy would catch her harried mother glancing contemplatively out the window, over the backyard, toward the blue mountains in the distance. Peggy would watch her mother quietly and wonder what she was thinking. Was she wistful for the days before she married Dad and started having children? Once, she had caught Peggy watching and shook her head.

"You have such silly notions, Margaret. I did not have a life before your father. He and you kids are my life. I just think those hills are awfully beautiful in the sunshine."

She then hurried to straighten out the pleats in the starched linen curtains and scuttled out of the room to tend to the laundry. Peggy supposed that Mama could have been telling the truth, but she always had this inkling that there was something her mother didn't say. Something that hid beneath the surface, something that Pine Sol and floor wax did not quite satisfy.

Peggy was so happy to be right there, alone in her little room, with her stack of books, her window overlooking the avenue, her little job in the big city, and a tingle in her spine that she was finally on her way to being the person she wanted to be. With the contented sigh of a cat stretching its back after a nap, Peggy stood and placed her empty China cup back in its saucer. She contemplated bringing the cup back down to the kitchen, as she knew that is what Mrs. Penske would prefer, but that seemed an awful long way to go when her narrow bed was right here. And besides, the landlady would come and take it in the morning after she left for work. Tossing her afghan into its usual heap on the window seat, Peggy turned out her lamp, pulled the curtains closed and shuffled to her bed. Snuggling under her three thin duvets, she considered that maybe she should have worn her afghan to bed, as well, for warmth. She set her eyes on the thin, yellow shaft of light that sliced across the floor from between the curtains and felt herself drift into a contented sleep.

2

The snow had landed heavily throughout the night and blanketed the streets and sidewalks. Cars slipped and spun as they attempted to navigate the white mass. Peggy picked her way carefully to the train station, linked arm in arm with Mary and Audrey. To passersby, the three girls made an adorable picture of youthful, pretty exuberance. Their cheeks were pink from the cold, their hands bemittened, their faces framed by curls and waves, and a cheery sparkle in their eyes. Audrey was the tallest of the three, and Mary, by far, the shortest. Interleaved was Peggy, average height and slim build. They walked as carefully as they could and giggled mercilessly at the girl who had the bad fortune to slip and fall. In fairness, each of the girls had her own turn to find herself flattened on the icy sidewalk and the object of mirth. When they reached the crossroads, they kissed and said their good days, and each headed off in her own direction. Mary, to the Women's College just two blocks away; Audrey, to Macy's, where she worked in the dress salon, and helped women with figures not at all like her own find The Dress of The Season; and Peggy, to the train station where she would read for the twenty-minute ride to the newspaper, where she worked as a typist.

At the station, Peggy handed over her two dimes to

the station master for her ticket and went to stand with the throng on the platform. The sky was grey and bright, no longer snowing, but clearly not ready to give up the idea that it might. She loved this part of the day. The part where she felt she belonged to something big. Here was a man in a thick woolen coat, hat, and leather gloves, holding a briefcase and glancing at the large clock across the track; there was a young man in an ill-fitting jacket, chatting animatedly with an older gentleman, who was attempting to read the morning paper. The paper thought Peggy, which I helped create. The impossible thrill this gave her was hard for her to describe. True, she was only a typist, in a typing pool full or other girls and women who spent their days in a smoke-filled room, clacking away on the heavy Olympias, and drinking paper cups of coffee from an old Landers electric percolator, which had probably been there since the advent of electricity. Peggy knew that it was only a matter of time before she was able to prove herself and become a writer. Lots of girls were junior copywriters, and she knew that they did a lot of writing, for none of the credit, and Peggy knew that wasn't for her. There were a couple of lady journalists at the paper, and she was determined that one day, there would be streams of articles with her byline. Peggy Anne Brennan. Or perhaps her Christian name would be more official – Margaret Anne Brennan. The truth was she despised the name Margaret. It was so old fashioned, so matronly. She felt Peggy was so much more youthful and pluckier. Giving her head a curt little nod, as though that decided the matter, although no one had asked her to give it any thought, Peggy stepped onto the newly arrived train and found a seat facing the middle aisle. Squeezing herself between an elderly woman all in black, and a young mother holding an infant on her lap, while trying to restrain two older children, who looked to be twins, from running the length of the car, Peggy smoothed out her coat and subtly tried to stamp a clump of snow from her boot. She was not having any luck, and then, suddenly the snow was freed and landed squarely on the shoe of the elderly lady, who eyed her suspiciously and then aggressively kicked the snow to the floor.

Peggy blushed, "I do apologise, ma'am. It was an accident."

Peggy gave the woman her most winning smile and then adjusted herself in her seat to face away from her, finding herself face to face with the drooling infant. Peggy sighed and settled in for what would surely be an uncomfortable journey.

"Miss Brennan, could I see you for a moment in my office?"

Mr. Latham appeared in the doorway of the typing pool. Peggy turned to see the older gentleman who had called her. She stood, adjusted her sweater and followed Mr. Latham down the hall.

"Please sit," he said, indicating to the two low leather chairs in front of his massive wooden desk. Mr. Latham sat in his impressive chair, while Peggy settled herself and crossed her ankles to the side, as these were very low chairs. Peggy wondered if Mr. Latham was trying to make a point by having his guests sit nearly on the floor, while he himself sat behind a desk that may as well have been a judge's bench.

"Miss Brennan, I would like to discuss with you your role here at the Tribune. You are aware that you have been hired as a typist, correct?"

Peggy was confused. Of course, she was aware. She hadn't been hired as a janitor, a receptionist, or a circus performer, for that matter.

"Why, yes, sir, Mr. Latham, of course."

"Good, good. I wanted to make myself perfectly plain, what is expected of you. You are to type the articles presented to you by the men who do the writing. Is that clear?”

Still baffled, Peggy nodded. Mr. Latham sat back ever so slightly in his chair.

“Good, good. It was brought to my attention by John Olson that perhaps you were thinking a bit beyond yourself.”

“Beyond myself, sir? I’m afraid I don’t understand.” Peggy watched as Mr. Latham took a slurp of his coffee, picked up a cigarette from the nearby ashtray, and attempted to puff on the no longer lit tube. He did not seem to notice, as he held it and smoothed out his mustache.

“Hmm... well, John... well, that is, Mr. Olson was sorting through the stack of articles that you typed this week and he came across something that he knows he did not write, and he knows that none of the other men around here would have written such a piece, and he started thinking that maybe you had it in your head to try your hand at writing. That isn’t so, now is it, Miss Brennan?”

With a frown, Peggy sat up straighter in her chair, “And if I have, what is it to Mr. Olson, sir? With all due respect, I am a very talented writer. I was first in my class at College and worked on our school’s paper. I don’t suppose that is of any interest to Mr. Olson, is it? He certainly can’t hope that I intend to simply be a typist for the rest of my days, can he?” Peggy was trying to maintain her composure, but her natural born temper made it challenging to do so. She felt her cheeks and ears become hot. She felt hot, angry tears begin to sting behind her eyes. She took a deep breath and lifted her pointed chin in what she hoped passed for an imperious look. She hated that when she was angry, tears pricked at her.

"Now, now, Miss Brennan, let's not get emotional. Of course, Mr. Olson does not intend to keep you as a typist for all time. Why one day, if you don't find yourself a husband just yet, he might even see fit to make you a secretary. So, don't you go getting all hot and bothered."

A secretary! Indeed, thought Peggy.

"I apologise, sir, but my ambition is not to be a secretary. In fact, I hope to have a secretary of my own someday when I am a writer of my own volition. I know I can do it. I know it will take time, and I am willing to work hard, but that's beside the point."

"Good, good. Well, I see that you have been reading that Betty Friedan's little book, too, haven't you? My wife read that recently and has been hardly bearable since. Well, you just keep your own writing to yourself, and remember, I am not paying you to write articles, and all that, I am paying you to type out the articles that real journalists write. Just keep that in mind, before you go getting yourself in any more trouble, you hear?"

It was hard to decide how to react to this situation. Peggy glanced toward the window and saw that the snow had begun to fall for the second time that day. She took a deep breath and reminded herself that she had worked too hard and saved for too long and gone against her parents' wishes to get this far. She was determined not to let one Feminine Mystique-fearing manager put her out onto the street.

"Yes, sir. I apologise for the mistake, sir. I will stick to the task at hand, sir. Is that all, sir?" Peggy blinked back the tears in her cunning green eyes and prepared to stand. All the "Good, gooding" and false politeness in the world were not going to stop her.

"Good, good. Yes, that's all Miss Brennan. I'm glad we understand each other."

"Indeed, sir."

"Good, good."

4

Sitting at a small café table a block away from the paper, Peggy lit a cigarette and took a deep inhale. Her hands shook, and her face still burned hot. She picked up the slim menu, holding the cigarette between her long, thin fingers. She was working to reconcile her conversation with Mr. Latham, or rather, Mr. Latham's character assassination of her. She would never be That Girl. The girl who gave herself away to the highest bidder, the one who would be wooed to the rambling house in Markham with the small children and the gleaming appliances, in a fashionable avocado or harvest gold, the one for whom a silver Pontiac Fairlane was an exciting purchase, the one for whom pushing a trolley in the shiny new supermarket was a fulfilling adventure. Her sisters, Joan and Linda, were those girls. Linda had married Tom fresh out of high school, without even letting the ink dry on her diploma. She had followed Tom to Chicago, where he had gotten a job working for HR McLucken Advertising. She spent her time cleaning her house and desperately hoping for a baby. After four years of marriage, and still no baby, there had been talk in the family about how happy their marriage truly could be. Mrs. Brennan spoke in hushed tones to her sister Joan, who had married John Michael after completing her Bachelor's Degree at the Women's College and had proceeded to produce a new child every two years for the last eight years, that "we both know how a woman can never truly fulfill herself, nor can she expect to keep her husband if she can't give him a baby!"

Joan had looked truly horrified at her mother's gossip but did nothing to refute the argument. Peggy had sniffed and left the room, feeling the eyes of both her sister and her mother on her as she went.

"Can I take your order, miss?"

"Please. I will take a coffee, two creams, two sugars; a tuna salad sandwich, toasted, and a small dish of the pickles. Thank you."

Peggy handed the menu back to the server, without glancing up. It was her habit to be more concerned with her own thoughts than with those whose job it was to serve her. She had read articles recently that those in the serving class were offended by being disregarded as merely part of the décor. It had given her pause, but that was all it gave her. She daintily placed her cigarette in the cut crystal ashtray on the table and looked out the large front window. She pursed her painted red lips and rested her chin in her hand and mulled. She would not give up her writing to please Mr. Latham; she would simply need to be subtler. She took a pen from her brown leather handbag and proceeded to make a list on a napkin, above the tiny golden sunshine that made the café's logo. First, she would purchase a small writing book to carry with her, so future lists and notes would not need to be scrawled on napkins; second, she would begin saving any money that did not go to her room and board, from her meager pay to purchase a portable typewriter. She had seen some truly dazzling models but knew that her budget would fall more in line with the used ones at the pawn shop near the river. Third, she would seek out the lady journalists at the Tribune and she would glean all the information she could from them; she would pick up their coats from the launders if that was what it took; fourth, she would continue jotting down her notes and thoughts, and sketches, and re-read the file of her writing so that she could improve and develop her voice. This last point caused Peggy to wrinkle her freckled nose and give a small smile, for she was certain that she did not need to improve her voice. She knew that given the chance, she would represent many, many girls like herself. She did not really see what she needed to be taught, however, she knew that it was best to at least appear to be working to improve oneself. She stirred her newly arrived coffee with the tiny silver spoon, engraved with the same delicate sunshine, and placed the napkin in her purse.

5

Peggy wound her scarf around her throat just slightly tighter. She could feel the wet warmth where her breath formed a dewy mark on the soft yarn. She knew that by the time she was kicking the snow off her boots on the front steps, there would be tiny ice crystals there. She wandered down the sidewalk, noticing that if the walks had been cleared at some point in the day, the ongoing flurries had filled them in again. Back home, the walks would have been a blanket of white, with a few footsteps quilting it at even recesses. The lamps would cast a soft yellow halo around the poles. Couples would walk slowly and stop to look in the shop windows, where Mr. Smith and Mr. Johannsen would have placed gleaming holly, complete with minuscule red berries, sprays of tinsel, and the "giftables", as Mr. Smith had coined in the 1930s, and which had become town slang in the ensuing years. Here, in the city, there were dozens of individuals, stomping through the snow, leaving messy piles of the stuff all over the street, bumping into one another, avoiding eye contact with each other and their umbrellas. Until now, Peggy had never seen anyone carry an umbrella to guard against snowflakes. While she waited to cross the busy intersection, she looked up and found herself blinking against the snowflakes. Before she remembered herself, she slipped her pink tongue past her lips and caught a few flakes on her tongue. A small chuckle from behind her shook her back to reality and she looked around, embarrassed to have been caught in such a blatant act of childhood fancy. She saw that the chuckle had come from a tall man, also waiting to cross. He had a handsome face, with a pleasant smile. He wore a coat, which judging from the cut had been expertly tailored to him, and more than likely cost a pretty penny. He wore a matching navy-blue hat, leather gloves, a soft grey scarf, and carried a supple black briefcase. Peggy tried to find something to say to hide her embarrassment, but her mind was blank. So, she poked out her chin and lifted her face, defying the man to mock her.

"You reminded me of my little sister. She was always doing that when we were children. She was almost as endearing as you, but not quite," said the man with a wink.

"Oh... well, ha-ha... it was just a moment of foolishness... I don`t... well, hmmm... well, it`s NOT polite to laugh at strange girls, I`ll have you know!" Her indignation belied the warm feeling in the pit of her stomach. She wasn't sure if it was pure discomfiture or that, mingled with a slight feeling of attraction to the handsome man before her.

"Oh, ho ho!" He chuckled again, "Well, I apologise for the offence, miss. Perhaps you will allow me to buy you a drink to make up for it? There is a little place just up the block that serves warm coffee if you will allow me to seek your forgiveness?" His eyes twinkled, and the edges of his lips twitched, in a clear attempt not to laugh again, and incur further wrath from the lovely pixie in front of him.

"Oh no, sir! Thank you, that's very kind of you, and I will grant you my forgiveness," she said while her own eyes twinkled, the bright green vivid as a cat's, "but I make it a rule to never go anywhere with strangers off the street. Have a good night."

Peggy glanced back at the street, and seeing no cars coming, darted out into the darkness, towards home, no longer concerned with slipping, or snowflakes, or managers. Her only thought was to make it to the dime store to purchase a journal and then to hurry home for the warmth of the fireplace in Mrs. Penske's den. She smiled to herself at the thought of the handsome gentleman. This was not the first man to have shown interest in her, as she was a striking girl, and she was not ashamed to know this regarding herself. Facts were facts. Peggy was clever, witty, and lovely. But what struck her was that this was the first man in the city of whom Peggy herself had also taken notice. He seemed to be not only handsome but to have been clothed as he was, he would have had to have been at least moderately successful. Her father had always told her that if she wanted to get ahead as a writer, she would need to find a collection of successful men with whom to align herself. She had scoffed at the thought. Men were always telling her that she would need a man to make the most of her life. But at the thought of the man at the intersection, she was, for the first time, curious about that idea of her father's.

Peggy turned left sharply at the corner and then slowed her pace. It was difficult to maintain the brisk pace on the slippery cement with the cold biting her eyes and burning her nose. With a tiny shake of her burnished head and a wrinkling of her freckled nose, Peggy walked through the extended rectangle of light pouring from the large picture window of the dime store and onto the road. In the dark, the light seemed to welcome passersby to the warmth within the shop. The little brass bells tinkled as Peggy pushed the heavy door into the store and stepped into the friendliness of the cozy store. Shelves surrounded her. Reaching to the ceiling along the outer walls of the store, the shelves seemed to offer every conceivable convenience and frivolity. The long, low counter at the back of the store held bins of penny candy, where two small children were deep in thought, working out which candies would give them the most pleasure for their tiny fortune. Each held two pennies almost as shiny as their young faces. Here and there throughout the store, spinning racks held colourful greeting cards, pantyhose, novelties, and sundries. Peggy wandered the store, as though she had no real purpose. As though she did not know what she wanted, and when a young woman asked her cheerfully if she needed help finding anything, Peggy absently answered that she was just browsing. She was content to find the journals own her own. She looked at the Shiny-Brite glass Christmas ornaments in their sparkly Technicolor. She passed jars filled with unsharpened pencils and pens, Pink Pearl erasers, and the racks of cowboy and romance novels favoured by those that Peggy felt were intellectually inferior to her. Her literary preferences were deeper, in her own not-so-humble opinion. Jack Kerouac, Allen Ginsberg, the Brontë Sisters, Jane Austen, Shelley, William Blake, Thoreau. These were the authors that Peggy felt everyone should sink their teeth into. Anything less was greeted by barely cloaked disdain. Her sisters had often told her that she was a snob about books, and that snobbishness was not an attractive trait in a woman. She would argue that she was not a snob; that she did not feel the need to disguise her intelligence to appear 'lady-like'.

She found a shelf; half tilted forward, bearing a variety of journals and notebooks. She decided that she would buy one of each. A notebook to record her thoughts and lists and essay ideas, and a journal to record the life she was living. Something to look back on, when she was a Pulitzer Prize winner. She could picture a faceless publisher begging her to publish the journal. Something that would be adored by young women like herself in the next generation. Young women who would not want to

be at home with adoring children and appliances.
She picked up a beautiful journal: small, and fat,
with bright blue leather binding, and shiny pink
Chinese-silk covering the front and back. Inside,
the pages were thin and delicate, almost
transparent. She clutched the journal and selected a
tiny spiral bound notebook, one like she had seen
in the hands of the serious journalists at the paper.
She wandered back to the pencils and selected a
tiny pencil, no longer than her pinky finger. She
would keep it slid through the gold-coloured spiral,
to keep it in place inside her handbag. With a faint
thrill, she carried her small prizes to the diminutive,
frizzy-haired man at the back counter.

6

The scent of the roast in the kitchen was dizzying up in Peggy's tiny room. She was torn between making the first mark in her new journal and running downstairs in her stockinged feet with the other girls, mouths watering to devour Mrs. Penske's famously delicious dinner. The sound of the small monster in her belly announcing its presence made her mind up for her. She grabbed her father's old grey cardigan off the end of her bed and shuffled along the smoothly waxed floor and down the three flights of stairs to the kitchen. She poked her head in to see that Mrs. Penske and her daughter, Anya, were sweating while running back and forth in the tiny steamy kitchen. There was a pan of boiled potatoes cooling on the counter, a bowl of roasted carrots and more potatoes. Anya was filling bowls with cabbage soup, and Mrs. Penske was pulling the large sizzling roast out of the oven. Peggy considered offering to help, but that thought lasted only a split second, and then she quietly backed out of the room, telling herself she would just be in the way. She meandered into the ample dining room and helped herself to one of the mismatched wine goblets on the table, and an overly large pour of the red wine set on the crocheted runner on the sideboard. While sipping the sour, plum-coloured liquor, she wrinkled her

23

nose, in part due to the alcohol and in equal measure due to disdain she held for the folksy charm of the off-white runner. She knew that when she was in her own home, she wouldn't settle for anything so outdated. She would have the cleanest whites, the most sparkling crystal, and the clearest surfaces. It did not occur to Peggy who would be keeping the whites so clean, nor the surfaces clear. Of all she was certain, she was certain it would not be her.

"Peggy Sue!!"

Rita entered the dining room, calling Peggy by her most dreaded nickname. Since the day Buddy Holly and the Crickets first sang that fateful tune, Peggy could never escape the moniker. Rita was a short, plump girl with florid taste in clothing and wore her peroxide blonde hair in an elaborate beehive. Today, the tower was bedecked with tiny pink ribbon bows, which almost matched the large pink paisley swirls on her knee-length acid yellow dress. Her long sleeves ending in elaborate bell cuffs, finished by pink ruffles. Her hose was garish lavender, and her patent white Mary Janes completed the image that was Rita. Peggy found Rita's appearance to be obscene, however, underneath the soaring tufts of blondeness, and the Twiggy eyeliner, Rita had a kindness unsurpassed by anyone that Peggy had ever met, which was the only reason that Peggy always let the "Peggy Sue" slide when it came from Rita. She knew it was meant as a term of endearment, and that no teasing was meant.

"Evening, Rita," Peggy smiled at her friend. "Going out tonight? You look like you are set to paint the town."

"Oh, good golly, no! This old thing? I had an interview at a groovy shop in the Village! Gotta dress the part after all!" Rita flashed Peggy an exaggerated wink and said, "Howsabout you pour me one a those?" nodding to Peggy's goblet.

"Sure thing," Peggy reached for the decanter, and asked "So? How was the interview? Why the Village? It's so far! You haven't got designs to leave us, have you?"

"Well, the interview was boss. The kids there are really groovy. I dug their vibe, ya know?" Peggy tried not to visibly shake her head at Rita's extensive use of slang. As a self-proclaimed writer and aspiring journalist, Peggy never "dug" anyone's "vibe". But Rita spoke like a true child of the times. "I dunno, though. You're right, it's real far, and I ain't interested in moving downtown. We both know I'd be the size of a blimp if I ate whatever I wanted, and that isn't what Ma is sending me to art school for. She keeps sending me little articles from Good Housekeeping on diets and losing weight. Next thing I know, she'll be sending me to fat camp. I mean, I know I don't gotta go, but you try sayin' no to Ma and see how far you get, ya know? She's got

over one another to get the One Man's attention.
His attention could seemingly make or break the
careers of all the other men. Peggy liked to see
them all watching to spot who would distinguish
himself amongst them before the meal was through.
She was sure that the one who held his own was the
one who would be made project manager of the
next ad campaign or would be promoted to Junior
Middle Vice President – Midwest Division. The
Waitress would seemingly float through the café or
diner or bar, with an encumbered grace. Her large
black or silver or mirrored tray would be balanced
perilously on one dainty wrist, while she
maneuvered past full tables, tipped back chairs and
the occasional unwarranted tap to her derriere.
Peggy could tell who had been The Waitress the
longest by how she responded to the undesired
attention of her male patrons. If she had been
working for a long time, she was often resigned to it,
and would give the face attached to the hand a wan
smile; if she had been working for a long time but
was still young enough to hope that one of these
lotharios would someday make good on the
promise that the tap incited, she would glance back
and give the man a cheeky wink and her most
seductive smile; if she was new to her role as The
Waitress, she would redden to the tips of her ears,
tip her chin down, and quickly, eyes downcast,
disappear behind the swinging doors, embarrassed
and shocked that anyone would think she was That
Sort of Girl. Turning her attention to The Host, a

resident not of diners or cafes, but rather the finer clubs and restaurants, Peggy would take note of his invariably slick hair, tailored black dinner jacket, crisp white collar and air of distinct superiority. His chin would be tipped up, allowing him to cast downward glances at all that dared to approach his podium, his glinting spectacles would balance precariously on his usually substantial nose, and he would be resting one hand on his reservation book, petting it as one would pet a beloved dog. What happened with the hand not resting on the Almighty Reservation Book was of the keenest interest to Peggy, as this was the hand that required the proverbial grease. Peggy made a game of guessing which patron would casually reach into his jacket pocket, slip a crisply folded bill of varying denomination into his hand, and then graciously extend that hand to The Host. The slip required sleight of hand, discretion and the correct Presidential face on the bill to have success. If the bill was over ten dollars, Peggy would see The Host shoot a meaningful glance at the Almighty Book, and then he would collect the required number of leather-bound menus and escort the patron to a table that was neither The Best Table in The House nor the worst. Peggy was always curious to know and had to restrain herself from approaching the palm-greaser to learn, how he whisked the money out so quickly. She assumed he must have had the bill artfully folded and ideally placed in the right pocket, to ease its travel into the right hand of

The Host. She smiled to herself, imagining a man fumbling in his pocket with his money clip. This could certainly not be the way. If the proffered bill was of any denomination above twenty dollars, The Host would, without hesitation direct the patrons, nay – his new best friend and company, to a chic booth in the corner, or depending on the patrons inclination to see and be seen, a gleaming table in the centre of the room, perhaps overhung by a gilt-framed mirror, allowing the guests at the table to steal discreet glances down the neckline of their lady's evening dress, while she remains none the wiser. Peggy was determined that she would never willingly sit at such a table, and if that seemed to be the way her date was headed, she would indignantly wear her coat, buttoned to the collar through the whole meal. There were certainly some things that her mother had taught her. The Bartender usually had the expression of a war-weary doctor, offering pints of beer, glasses of wine and cocktails in lieu of prescriptions. Peggy noticed that those who sat right at the bar, on the high stools, near the booze, the peanuts, and The Bartender, had the most desperate look to them. They had not come to enjoy the atmosphere; they had come to not go home. After a drink or two have loosened their lips and warmed their tongues, they would begin to confide in The Bartender. Peggy was sure that if anyone should be writing a gossip column for the daily papers, it ought to be The Bartenders. She could think of almost no one who had the inside "scoop" on more members of the community than did they. Priests, doctors, hairstylists and The Bartender – holders of infinite knowledge, infinite patience, and a level of empathy that allowed them to return day, after day, after day to their miserable charges. The Harried Mothers and The Small Children were most often, quite literally, hand in hand. In a café, Peggy would observe a woman whose hair was too frizzy, her hat was askew, her coat did not quite fit any longer – either too tight from weight not yet lost, or too loose for weight never again found. The Harried Mothers would hastily gulp their tea, or coffee, or rarely cocktail, while they attempted to keep The Small Children occupied with a glass of milk or a milkshake or a pastry. If she had a babe in arms, she would be the World's Smallest Juggling Act – gently rocking the baby, swigging her coffee, most certainly burning the roof of her mouth in the process, keeping the Small Children in their seats by hissing through gritted teeth "Sally! Please! This is a restaurant! Must you behave like a savage? What would your father say?" absent-mindedly brushing crumbs from Sally/Tommy/Susan's cake, which had landed on Gracie/Georgie/Dickie's forehead. Peggy loathed thinking that her own dear Joanie was most likely one of these Harried Mothers when she was out with her brood of four. She was further disturbed by the thought that poor Linda felt desperate that she should become such a woman. How could she be willing to give up a nice leisurely biscuit, a cut-glass bowl with dainty gherkins and a cup of coffee that did not scald the inside of her mouth? Peggy felt that although she could observe them and have a splendid time on her own doing so, she most certainly could never become one. The very idea, she would shiver at the thought.

Peggy peeked out the window of her little bedroom. Still snowing. She wound her scarf a little more tightly around her neck and headed for the door. She could hear Rita at the bottom of the stairs, putting on her bright red boots, and chatting animatedly with Emily and Audrey. To say that Rita spoke a mile a minute would be an understatement. As she descended, Peggy smiled to herself to see her three friends. Rita doing the talking whilst Em and Audie, nodded and tutted at appropriate intervals.

"Hiya, girls," said Peggy, entering the fray.

"Good morning, sunshine! It's gonna be another cold one! Betcha Mrs. Penske is gonna be complainin' about the cost of heating this joint by dinner!" Rita grinned with mischievous pleasure at the anticipated diatribe she was almost certain would occur upon their seating at the supper table.

"Rita!" exclaimed Audrey, "To speak so about our landlady! Your mother would just fall down dead if she heard you!"

"Nah! My ma woulda said the same thing. We ain't so good at keepin' things in our heads. What's gonna come out is gonna come out! 'Sides, I ain't said nothin' that Old Lady Penske wouldn't a said herself." Rita flashed her charming grin, today lacquered in a deathly lilac lipstick. Peggy couldn't help but think that it was a tad on the morbid side, but as always, kept that thought to herself. Kissing her friends quickly, as they stumbled out into the cold morning, Peggy wished that she had not ignored her alarm clock and had gone down for a nice hot cup of coffee and maybe some toast. Mornings were not her strong suit. Peggy was a born night owl. A flashlight under the covers, reading until well past a decent hour, Peggy would never be the first Brennan girl out of bed. She told herself she couldn't sleep, but the truth was that she just loved the night. She loved the quiet; she loved to be alone with her thoughts. Her sisters used to complain that her light was keeping them up, and to for goodness' sake, Margaret Anne, just shut your eyes. Peggy would grouse that even if she shut her eyes, she would never fall asleep. So, she learned to wait. She would feel Joanie start to relax, and her breathing steady, and then shortly after that, she would hear Linda's gentle snoring from the narrow bed by the door. Being the youngest, Peggy would desperately wish that it was she, and not Linda, the oldest who could have a bed to herself. Mrs. Brennan would tell her that one day, Lin would move out and Peggy could have her bed, but in the meantime, to just appreciate that Joanie was there to warm the bed for her. Peggy would sigh, knowing that there was no use arguing with her mother. Once she heard the sounds of her sisters' sleep, she would creep out of bed, careful to avoid the creaky springs at the centre of the shared bed and pulling her beloved afghan from the foot of the bed, would slink to the window and cocoon herself between the radiator and the window ledge. From that spot, the streetlamp in front of the house shed just enough light and the Afghan and the radiator kept her warm, and she could read. Propping a book on her knees and resting her Dad's old army flashlight in her lap, Peggy would slip into her own, waking dream world. She learned to tell the time by the sounds in her suburban home. She and her sisters would go to bed around 9:30, to get their prescribed 'beauty sleep', then around 10:00, she would hear her father's heavy tread past her door; her mother would follow shortly after, after her she ensured that the coffee pot was set for the morning, that she was certain that she wiped the counters, the iron was definitely unplugged, the oven was off, the cat was let out, the back storm door was fastened, the shoes were neatly lined by the front door. Once the house had passed her inspection, Mrs. Brennan would take her hand knitted cloth, hang it over the kitchen sink faucet, and shut of the light. With a small nod of approval, Mrs. Brennan would murmur to herself, 'There. The kitchen is closed'. Peggy could see the routine in her mind's eye. Mama would never have left a single coffee grind on her gleaming Formica. When Peggy would hear the lights click off through the house, she knew that everyone was heading to bed. Without fail, even when her mother was in bed with the flu, Mrs. Brennan never passed her children`s bedrooms without coming in to check that all were safe and sound. Peggy would flick off her flashlight, as her mother quietly opened the door. She watched as her mother smoothed Linda`s hair, tugged Joan`s quilt higher over her shoulder, and then approached her.

"Come on, my pet. Time for sleep," Mrs. Brennan kissed Peggy`s unruly hair and held out her hand to take the book.

In her room, now, Peggy missed having her mother come to send her to bed. More than once, since moving to the city, Peggy would find herself dozing on her window seat, certainly hours past when she should have turned in. She did not really have any form of insomnia; she just had a love of quiet, peace and reading just one more chapter. There were some comforts that were given up trying her luck with freedom. Peggy ambled along the snow-ridden sidewalk, in the general direction of the train. She watched her friends giggle and tease each other. She wondered if they ever missed home or their mothers, or their brothers and sisters. She figured they must, but they were much better at keeping their sadness to themselves, she thought. But then, did they know how sad she sometimes felt? How nostalgic for the comforts of home? For the sound of Dad coming home at 5:30 on the nose, for the comfort of Mother's cool hand to the cheek when they were running a fever, for the comfort of knowing that no matter how angry Sister made you, she would be there to comb out your hair and listen after a dinner date gone awry, for the knowledge that Brother would always come to pick you up at the library if your study date ran long. Peggy did, now and then.

Shaking her head, to clear the cloud of wistfulness, Peggy began to think about her day to be. She remembered that she had to finish typing Mr. Olson's loathsome piece on Vice-President Humphrey and his Vietnam goals. She detested reading, or hearing, or typing, for that matter, anything that had to do with that awful war. She did not understand that war, and things that she did not understand tended to strike her as dull or ridiculous. That's not to say Peggy was unintelligent or ill-informed. She wasn't, she just preferred things she understood. She was hopeful that she would be tasked with typing work for one of the other writers, today. A sign of good faith, that perhaps she would be moving ahead in her career. That she would escape the typing pool in due course. Peggy never expected to jump the queue to her gleaming, solid oak desk, in a bright corner office, with a crystal ashtray, and a vase full of fresh, cut flowers, but she was always hoping for signs that she could view as mile markers in her mind. She sighed doubtfully. More than likely, she would type the dreary war piece, and then re-type the edited piece from yesterday, or perhaps the day before. Ad infinitum.

Sitting at her typewriter, Peggy delicately tapped her cigarette into the cheap ashtray and glanced up at the dirty windows. There was a constant layer of fug floating above the typing pool, due to the girls' cigarette smoke, and the pipe and cigar smoke wafted down the hall from the offices. It created a dreamy haze that Peggy could find herself lost in. She knew that Mother would be scandalized to see her puffing away on a cigarette, as it is simply not done. Oh, Mama, you're such an old fuddy-duddy, Peggy thought to herself. She looked over the sheet of paper that she had just finished typing, scanning scrupulously for any missed letters or typographical errors of any sort. A girl could lose her job for less than perfect, and Peggy, as much as she felt longing for her family at intervals, was determined that she would never go home, tail between her legs, to marry some tedious Everyman, and have millions of babies with dirty faces, pulling at her skirts and begging for more milk. Content that she had finished, she placed the article in the out basket, from whence the young mail boy would snatch it, and bring it down to Copy. Peggy stood and wandered somewhat aimlessly through the small desks to the ancient coffee urn and poured herself a brimming cup. She grimaced when she saw that there would be no room for her splash of cream and lumps of sugar. She despised black coffee, but she could see no other option than to sip until there was room. An unconscious look of utter disgust clouded her features, as she forced the hot drink down.

"Not good, eh?"

Startled, Peggy turned around to find the same man behind her. The man from the corner. What was he doing here? For a moment it crossed her mind that he had followed her, but she passed that off as inconceivable, as it had been days since he had caught her in her moment of playfulness. And besides, she hadn't gone to work after that, she was sure that she had been heading home at that time.

"Nope. Just terrible. But I'm afraid I overfilled my cup and haven't room for cream and sugar. Making this malicious brew even more challenging to swallow," Peggy answered ruefully; still suspicious as to why the man was here.

"Well, if it's that bad, I must speak to your manager about getting you some better coffee. I'd hate to think of you working away, day in and day out on crummy coffee," said the man with a sparkle in his eye.

"Oh no! I wouldn't dream of it. I am determined to thrive at this job. It is a steppingstone, you know. I wouldn't dare complain about something as trivial as lousy coffee. Now, why am I telling you all of this? I don't even know you! I apologise for going on, sir."

"Well, I beg to differ, Miss. I am sure we are already acquainted. I daresay we met a few nights ago. In the snow? You were in a hurry to get somewhere, as I recall," the man teased.

"Oh. Yes. Of course. You do remember, then. Whatever are you doing here? If I didn't know any better, I'd say you were following me!" Peggy caught herself flirting ever so slightly. What was it about this man?

"If only, Miss..." the man trailed off, indicating that Peggy should introduce herself.

"Brennan. Peggy Brennan."

"Miss Brennan. But unfortunately, my reasons for being here aren't nearly as pleasing as that. I am here to start work. I have been made the assignment editor and am just wandering to get the lay of the land. Finding you was merely a happy coincidence."

"Assignment editor? Huh. I thought Mr. Tennant was Assignment editor."

"He was. But unfortunately, Mr. Tennant has decided to head for greener pastures. He was hired as Senior Editor at the Times, so it was determined that I would replace him." The way the man said that last part made Peggy cock her head with interest. There was something desolate about the way he had said it. But who would possibly be melancholy about such a wonderful position? Peggy herself would simply jump at the chance to attach Assignment Editor to her name. Peggy Anne Brennan, Assignment Editor. Before she had time to realize how far ahead of herself, she was getting, another typist popped over and said that Mr. Olson was looking for her. Peggy took her leave and walked away, stopping momentarily to place her cup on her desk, before rapping smartly on Mr. Olson's office door.

"Miss Brennan. I thought maybe you gave up and abandoned us. You know I would be lost without you," Mr. Olson looked at her with a meaningful look.

It was a look Mr. Brennan had given her often if he felt she was lollygagging or wasting her time when she should be doing something productive. The look made Peggy feel immediately wrong-footed and ill at ease.

"No, no, sir. I was just getting a cup of coffee. I wasn't gone but a minute. Mr.... erm, well, I didn't catch his name, but the new assignment editor was asking me for some information about the typing pool." Peggy knew this was a bit of a fudge, but she had the feeling that Mr. Assignment Editor wouldn't rat her out. Besides, why would Mr. Olson check anyway?

"The new assignment editor? Oh, yes, Mr. Grant. I forgot he would be here today. Mind you stay out of his way. Don't be asking him to start assigning you stories, now." Peggy checked to see if Mr. Olson was kidding, but from what she could tell, Mr. Olson was completely sincere. Peggy was taken aback by his expression.

"Ummm... no, of course not, sir. I, erm, I wouldn't think of it," Peggy tried to keep a cool head, but in her heart of hearts, she knew that one day, in the not-too-distant future, she would do exactly that. "Is that everything? Or did you need anything else?"

"Oh, yes. Of course, I do need something. The Nam story – finish that up pronto. Howards is breathing down my neck. Get it out by 2:30."

"Mr. Olson, I completed that before I went for my coffee. I wouldn't have dreamed of breaking for coffee without beating a deadline," Peggy said, emphasizing the word beating. She was determined to make a name for herself at The Tribune, and by being indispensable, she saw her best opportunity.

"Did you, now?" Mr. Olson looked pleased for the first time in their encounter. Peggy thought it was likely that it was the first time he had looked pleased all day. Maybe even all month. Looking at the faded black and white portrait of a Mrs. Olson of days gone by, Peggy thought, not for the first time, that she did not envy the woman. "Lovely, alright, then that's all. Back to work with you now."

<h1 style="text-align:center">10</h1>

Mr. Grant. Peggy mused that at least she now had a name. She thought the name was suitable. She was curious as to his given name, but for now, at least she could stop thinking of him as The Man. She pushed the boiled peas and carrot cubes around on her plate. She remembered the glint in his eye as he talked about the coffee. She thought what a lovely face he had. Handsome, and kind, but not too handsome; he was likable. She didn't like men who were too handsome. It made her terribly uncomfortable. She felt at a loss for words and Peggy did not enjoy that. There had been a boy back home, tall, dark hair, shockingly blue eyes, and a strong jaw. He had been too much for her. She remembered when he would pass her, she would blush; if he ever spoke to her, however mundane the topic, she couldn't bear it. Some of her old girlfriends had crushed on him, each proclaiming that they would be Mrs. Blue Eyes, but not Peggy. Peggy could not stand to think of what a conversation with him would have been. He would perhaps talk about his day, and Peggy would simply look at the ceiling, hoping to avoid his piercing gaze. Mr. Grant, on the other hand, was someone she felt she could talk to. When she had met him, in both instances, she did not feel any sense of alarming tongue-tiedness. She had spoken her mind each time.

"Peg?" Peggy glanced up at Mary across the table from her with a start. "Yes? Sorry, were you talking to me?"

"The peas, babe, could you pass the peas?"

"Right! Yes, of course!" Peggy picked up the ceramic dish of boiled and buttered peas and passed it across to Mary, with an over brightness.

"Daydreaming?" asked Emily, nudging Peggy's left elbow with a laugh.

"Ummm... no, not exactly. I was thinking about the new editor at the paper. He just started today, and I met him at the coffee urn. The strange thing is that I have seen him before."

"Once upon a dream?" teased Rita, in reference to Sleeping Beauty, the Disney movie that she knew Peggy adored from her childhood.

"NO!" Peggy laughed, "On the corner, in a snowstorm the other night. I was walking from the station, and we were both at the same light."

"Well? Tell us about him!" exclaimed Audrey, leaning forward in her chair.

"There isn't anything to tell. He's just a man who works at the paper! I just thought it was strange that I had met him before. That's all," Peggy finished lamely and looked down at her plate for a moment and peered under her lashes to see if the girls had gone back to their suppers.

"No one drowns their peas and carrots in gravy for

ten minutes, without taking a bite, if she has nothing to tell! There must be something?"

"Well, he seems nice. He told me he would get better coffee for the typing pool. His name is Mr. Grant. That's all there is."

"Mr. Grant? Ugh! He sounds old! If Peggy Sue was gonna be keen on anyone, it wouldn't be no Mr. Grant!" exclaimed Rita, dunking her heavily buttered bread into the pool of gravy on her plate.

The rest of the girls laughed at this, and the conversation drifted away to other things. Emily discussed her latest conversations with Teddy, Rita talked about the new shop in the village, Audrey ate her supper in quick silence, as she had a date with a new beau. It made Peggy laugh because Audrey made a habit of eating her supper quickly before her dates, even if she was going for a dinner date because she did not want to appear like a "ravenous cow" to her new gentleman. Peggy thought that a ravenous cow seemed like an odd analogy as she could not recall ever thinking of cows as particularly ravenous. Plodding was more cow-like to her mind. Nevertheless, Audrey devoured her dinner and then was able to appear dainty and neat at the restaurant. Peggy wondered what would happen when she eventually married one of these suitors and they realized that Audrey did, in fact, eat food like a normal woman. Peggy took a sip of wine from her cut-glass goblet and thought about what Mr.

Olson had said. She ought not to ask Mr. Grant for an assignment, but what if he should happen to decide himself to assign her a story. All she had to do was write one piece, which would undoubtedly be published in The Tribune. She had no concerns about that. And once it was published, they would all see what a capable writer she was. They would flock to her for the best pieces. Perhaps not right away. She knew she would have to earn her stripes, but in short order, she was certain, she would have her byline.

After supper, once Audrey had received approval that her slim fitting red dress was just the right shade, and certainly, as becoming as it had been in the change room at Macy's, Peggy ascended to her quiet room. She sighed a comforted breath, as she slipped out of her thick tights, and dark pink woolen camp skirt. She neatly hung the skirt in her wardrobe and then her heavy cable knit pullover. Her underthings she placed in her fine washables bag, to be washed and hung in the bathroom with the other girls' brassieres, panties, nylons, stockings, and girdles. She slipped her warm, Mama-made flannelette nightie over her head, stuffed her feet into her slippers and sat down at the window. She pulled the pins from her hair, one by one, tossing them onto the seat, at her feet, intending to put them back in her toiletries kit before bed, but knowing in the back of her mind that they would still be right there, other than the couple that fell to

the floor, when she awoke in the morning. Once
the last pin was removed, she scratched her scalp
and felt the luxuriousness of the moment. It always
felt so good to strip off the day, and finally be
home, in her nightgown, and her hair curling
around her shoulders. The excess hairspray would
crackle, as she worked to separate the strands.
Peggy scrunched her nose to fight back the
immediate tears that formed when she caught her
fingers in a tangle of hair, then, drawing another
deep breath, she leaned her forehead against the
ice-cold glass and looked down to the street. The
miniature moon glows from the headlamps of a
passing Oldsmobile briefly brightened the street,
and the snowflakes appeared to dance upwards as
they were buffeted in the air. She watched a couple
stroll arm in arm down the sidewalk, imagining a
life for them. He was Joe College, and she was Susy
Sunshine. He was lettering in track and field, and
she was a cheerleader. He ran the distance as she
stood on the sidelines with her curly brunette
ponytail bouncing off her shoulders, cheering him
on. Now they were heading to a movie, Peggy
thought. He would take her to see Doctor Zhivago,
and she would spend the entire three hours and
twenty minutes holding his hand, eyes rapt on the
screen, imagining that she was Lara, and he was
Yuri. He would buy her popcorn and licorice
whips, and she would daintily pick at them popcorn
and chew but one licorice whip. As Joe and Susy
turned the corner, Peggy blinked her eyes. She

thought – him, running; her, cheering from the
sidelines – how apt. This would be how Joe and
Susy would most likely be in a marriage. He would
go to work, figuratively running the distance,
whether a marathon or a sprint and she would
remain at home, permanently sidelined. With a
shiver, Peggy withdrew from the glass and tucked
her feet underneath her nightgown. She dug around
under the cobalt and rusty orange pillows lining the
window seat and pulled out the little journal that she
had purchased the night she had first met Mr.
Grant. She had taken to hiding it when it wasn't in
her hands. She couldn't say why, exactly, as it was
not a diary. It was just a book of story ideas and
thoughts; yet somehow, these thoughts seemed too
personal to leave lying about her room. She knew
that any of the girls might wander in and
absentmindedly flip it open, not knowing the
intrinsic value that Peggy placed on the sheaf of
papers within. She feared Anya or Mrs. Penske may
move it, and that she would never feel the same
connection to it; that the sanctity of the thing would
be destroyed. Finally, her fingers caught the corner
of the little book, and she drew it to her chest. She
plucked the pen from within and began to write her
thoughts about Joe College and Susy Sunshine, and
the sadness that swept her at the idea of Susy being
forever a cheerleader in the life of Joe and never
knowing the fulfillment of making a life of her own.
She wrote and wrote and wrote, pausing now and
again to stretch her fingers or rub the pad between

her left thumb and forefinger. She was grateful to dear old Dad for not allowing the teachers to force her into right-handedness. She imagined that all her creativity was released when she had the freedom to be herself. She knew of cases where children were forced into right-handedness and developed terrible stutters, and lifelong insecurities. Peggy wondered if her left hand was the reason for her independent streak, the reason she did things the hard way. Whatever the reason, Peggy was grateful.

Peggy was amid a swirl of pink taffeta, and blue chiffon, and canary yellow lace. She fingered the delicate material and looked around. She caught sight of Emily, near the rear of the department.

"Em!"

"Peggy! Darling!! You'll never guess! I have the biggest news!!" Emily's face was glowing. Her hair was smoothed back from her face and held in place with a wide, red satin ribbon. Her dark brown eyes were bright, as though lit from the inside. She was smiling so widely that she looked like a girl from a toothpaste ad.

"Alright, Hun, I'll bite. What's the news?" Peggy knew all too well what the news would be, she simply couldn't fathom why they must be in the dress department at Bloomingdale's for it.

"Peg, he did it! Teddy got the position in Chicago! He's going to be the Junior Accounts Director at Laurel, Laurel and Stanley! Isn't it the most?"

Peggy was flabbergasted. She was confused. She had been certain that Em was going to tell her that Teddy had finally decided to pick up his feet and pop the question. But leaving town? Moving hundreds of miles away? Becoming a Junior Accounts Director for what sounded like a vaudeville act? Why on Earth was Emily so excited?

Emily must have noticed the crease form on Peggy's brow, and the questioning look appear in her eyes, because her face lost a touch of its sheen, and she reached for Peggy's hands.

"Why honey! What's the matter? You knew Teddy was gunning for that position. I'm sure I've mentioned it at least a hundred times!"

"Well, sure, kid, but I thought you were going to tell me he'd finally gotten around to proposing, not that he was leaving the city! I mean, I knew he wanted the job, but I thought he wanted you more!" Peggy squeezed Emily's hands ever so slightly.

"Oh gosh! Peggy, you are a goose! You are such a darling for worrying about me, but you really mustn't. Why I was just getting to the good part! Now, he hasn't actually proposed yet, but he told me that he was going to head West to get settled, and find a place, and get set up in his new job, and then in a year, we would have a big old wedding, and then I will head out to join him, just as soon as I finish my teaching certificate!" The smile danced back onto Emily's face, her bright red lips just exactly matching the red of the ribbon. Peggy smiled back at her, but she had an uneasy feeling that things were not going to go as planned. She had a feeling that perhaps once Teddy was away from Emily, he would find that the relief from the

pressure of marriage would be too great, and he
might just extend his year, bit by bit.

Teddy was not a fellow of great backbone, and
Emily did hold onto him awfully tightly. But she was
determined that her negative thoughts would not
undermine Emily's happy ones.

"Ah, well that clears things up! So, what are we
doing here, in this overgrown confectionary?" Peggy
swept her hand around her, indicating to the candy-
coloured gowns that surrounded her.

"Well, Ted is going to take me dancing on Saturday
night, to celebrate the news. And he said that I
ought to buy something new, something befitting the
soon-to-be wife of an Executive." Peggy was sure that
Em said an executive with a capital E, as though it
was a proper noun in and of itself and worthy of its
own place in the world. "Mr. Laurel, the younger
Mr. Laurel, mind you, not the original Mr. Laurel,
that Mr. Laurel is in Chicago, but this Mr. Laurel
and his wife, Mrs. Laurel, have invited us for
cocktails on Saturday evening, and Teddy said he
just had to show me off and it was absolutely, one
hundred percent imperative that I make a good
impression with Mrs. Laurel. So here we are!
You're going to help me find just the right gown for
the night. I absolutely must make the right
impression. After all, if Mrs. Laurel takes a shine to
me, then she will be my ticket into the society in
Chicago, and anyone who is anyone needs the

correct introduction." Emily continued babbling incessantly about the importance of her role as Teddy's wife in the advancement of his career, and how she would be working so hard to make just the right impression, and what a great opportunity this was for the both of them, and on, and on and on, ad infinitum. Peggy nodded along, and made approving sounds when necessary, following Emily through the racks, as their arms became loaded down with more yards of fabric than most women would ever see in their lifetimes. At one point, Peggy caught sight of the price tag of one of the gowns and blanched. Two whole months' salary into one frock? The thought astounded her. Even if she wanted to spend that amount on a dress, she was sure her own purse would bite her hand if she tried to withdraw that amount of money from it. After several minutes of foraging, a perky young sales assistant approached them. She wore the standard sleek black wrap dress and her hair in a low bun at the nape of her neck.
Peggy noticed that even her shoes were sleek, with a low vamp, and a sensible mid-height heel, made of lustrous black satin.

"Hello ladies!" she chirped, "My name is Eliza, may I start you a fitting room?" She started reaching for the armloads of gowns.

"Please!" nodded Emily vigorously and then began to relay her story about Teddy and the Laurels, and the dancing, and the cocktails, to a grinning Eliza. Peggy felt a certain level of respect for this young girl

– she did not once appear to be distracted, and she genuinely seemed interested in what Em was sharing. It suddenly occurred to Peggy that maybe that was because this was what Eliza was hoping would happen to her one day. She would meet her Executive Prince, be swept up in a romance, which was paved in green, purchase an armload of gowns on his account, and live happily ever after, hoovering in her stilettos, and setting aside pin money for a new straw purse. Peggy followed wordlessly, inhaling deeply through her nose, and trying her best to remain interested in what was sure to be a dull day. In her imaginings on the way to Bloomingdale's, she thought she would meet Emily, they would shriek excitedly about the ring, and then cross the street to Tony's, where they would sip Manhattans and discuss bridal colours. Not that she had the least interest in bridal colours, but she had been present for Joanie and Linda's bridal preparations, and she could feign interest enough to get them through a cocktail. Simply because she found marriage dreadfully dull did not mean she could not be enthusiastic for other girls.

"Are you going to try anything, dear?" asked Eliza, with a genial smile. Peggy despised being called dear by women her own age unless they were chums. And while Eliza and Em may be chummy at the moment, Peggy was sure this would be the last time the elegant salesgirl and she would be in the same room. With an imperious gaze, Peggy replied that she would not, in fact, be trying on anything, and turned to settle herself on the tufted, purple velvet sofa that faced the fitting rooms. She had just settled her square, avocado Naugahyde purse on the seat beside her, and picked up a copy of Cosmopolitan from the shiny chrome and Formica table in front of her when she heard a soft chuckle just behind her. She spun so quickly in her seat that her carefully placed purse tumbled to the floor. As she tried to reach for it, while looking behind her, she found herself facing Mr. Grant. Fumbling around on the floor near her feet, she was aghast.

"Why, Mr. Grant! You simply must learn to stop sneaking up behind poor, unsuspecting ladies! At this rate, you shall give me gray hairs before my twenty-fifth birthday!" She felt her pale cheeks colour, the warmth spreading from the bridge of her nose to the tips of her ears. Finally, she caught the Lucite handle of the bag between the tips of her fingers, and raised herself to a proper sitting position, keeping the purse neatly in her lap for the time being.

"Ha! I quite agree, Miss Brennan, although I think your hair is several shades away from gray at this point. I shouldn't worry if I were you. I see that you have become acquainted with my name since our last meeting." Mr. Grant winked at her. Peggy was incensed. To be winked at by a man who was her superior at the paper. He would never take her work seriously if he thought she was the type of girl who tolerated winking. She lifted her chin and turned her back to him, cheeks burning with irritation in conjunction with her humiliation.

"Have I offended you, Miss Brennan?" Mr. Grant rounded the sofa, and sat comfortably down, not two feet from her.

"Well, I should say not, why should you assume that I am offended? Simply because I do not cotton to a man treating me as a child, does not by any stretch of the imagination indicate that I am offended."

Chin still lifted at an angle, she tilted her head, ever so slightly to the left, to see how he had received her barb. The man's eyes sparkled in amusement, and he rested his elbow on the arm of the sofa, hiding his mouth with his forefinger, cupping his chin with his thumb. His shoulder shook ever so slightly. Peggy was certain that Mr. Grant was laughing silently, and at her expense. She was about to take him to task for this inappropriate behaviour when Emily and Eliza came giggling out of the fitting rooms. Emily was covered from neck to toe in the lightest of blue French lace. The lace wrapped around her throat in a mock turtleneck, puffed at the sleeves, encircled her arms to her wrists, was tucked neatly at an empire waist, and then straight to the floor. It was incredibly stiff, and Peggy's eyes widened in what could only be perceived as horror. Before she could speak, Eliza beamed and rushed to Mr. Grant.

"John! Darling! How sweet of you to come! I'll be off in half an hour, and we can go to Tony's for drinks!" Mr. Grant stood, and kissed Eliza's cheeks, smiling back at her with affection. Peggy stiffened. She felt her face freeze in a polite smile and stared at the couple for a moment before she realized that Emily was trying to catch her eye.

"Well? What do we think? I feel like it is ever so sophisticated and powder blue really is my colour, after all. Do you think Teddy will like it? More importantly, do you think Mrs. Laurel will like it? After all, I simply must make a good impression on her." Em tugged at the left wrist of the gown and cocked her head beseechingly in the three-way mirror. Her eyes found Peggy's and Peggy wrinkled her nose.

"Ummm... well, the colour is darling on you, but, oh, I don't know... is it perhaps a tad... boring?"

"Boring? Do you think? Hmmm... maybe..." Emily turned this way and that, keeping her eyes on herself in the mirror. She appraised her figure in the frock and with a curt nod, started back for the fitting room, calling to Eliza, "let's try the periwinkle next." Eliza turned from Mr. Grant and hurried after Emily. Mr. Grant flopped himself back into his seat with a smile, sliding the sofa several inches back in the process. Peggy gripped the armrest in surprise. She shot him a look.

"Yes, I definitely agree with you. Unless that girl is to be the mother of the bride, that dress was much too boring. What's the occasion?" Mr. Grant asked off-handily, glancing at Peggy briefly.

"She is going to meet her boyfriend's new boss and his wife. She's intent on marrying him and wants to make the right impression," Peggy sniffed. She realized too late that she was being rather rude to the man who had the ability to help her forward her career at the paper and tried to remind herself that there was a fine line between being taken seriously as a journalist and being downright obstinate to the Assignment Editor. She changed her tone, "You and the salesgirl seem congenial." Peggy spoke brightly as though this was only a passing thought, nothing that concerned her, but simply idle chitchat.

Mr. Grant raised his right arm and slicked his forelock back, although it had not moved from its place in his smooth, Brylcreemed style.

"Yes, Eliza is a sweet girl. I am looking forward to my evening with her. So, your friend plans to marry her boyfriend's new boss and intends to make a good impression, right there, in front of his wife? That seems a bit brazen, don't you think?"

"What? What do you mean?" Peggy was genuinely confused at this train of thought.

"You said a moment ago that she was intent on marrying him and wanted to make the right impression."

"Well, certainly you knew that was not what I meant! She wants to marry Teddy, her boyfriend, and wants to make a good impression on Mr. and Mrs. Laurel, his boss and his boss' wife." Peggy shook her head and then noticed again that Mr. Grant was chuckling. The man was infuriating.

Emily and Eliza returned in a swirl of hot pink gauze.

"Well, the periwinkle was a bust, but what do you think of this?" Emily asked, beatifically. The colour was abhorrent, was what Peggy thought. She looked like a flamingo. A neon flamingo hanging above the entrance to a gaudy nightclub. Peggy was beginning to question her friend's taste, and potentially her sanity when Mr. Grant came to her rescue.

"If you will pardon my intrusion, from the male perspective, why not try something like that?" he pointed to the mannequin on a small pedestal to the left of the mirrors. It was a floor-length black gown, sewn all over with silver and black sequins. With a sweetheart neckline and knee-high slit on the right side, the sleeveless gown was a marvel.

"Oh no! I simply couldn't! My figure? That gown? I appreciate your insight, sir, but I don't think that is a look that I could pull off." Emily shook her dark head sadly and gestured to her ample bosom and wide hips.

"If you don't mind my saying so, that gown was

made for a figure like yours." Mr. Grant gave her a knowing, though not an inappropriate smile. Eliza nodded in agreement, although Peggy was fairly certain that anything that Jawwwwn said would be perfectly wonderful in Eliza's estimation.

"Well..." Em looked uncertain, but she gave a slight shrug, and Eliza snatched the same gown off the rack and hurried Emily back into the fitting room. Peggy had to admit that the gown was eye-catching. Mr.

Grant had nice taste. She was sure that Teddy would be thrilled to see Emily in something so daring, yet not too revealing.

"You have good taste, Mr. Grant," Peggy said approvingly.

"Miss Brennan, I think that is the first compliment I have heard from you," Mr. Grant looked pleasantly surprised at the change of tone.

"Well, we have only met thrice. One could hardly assume we would be speaking comfortably yet, Mr. Grant," Peggy was proud of herself for using 'thrice'. She was certain that as an editor, he would approve of the use of what her father called "twenty-five cent words".

"This is true. I think we will be able to remedy that, now that we shall be working in proximity," Mr. Grant said.

"Yes, I do hope so. Maybe I will be promoted to secretary one day, and I can sit in on some of your

very exciting meetings, taking notes or something,"
she said solemnly.

"Oh no, I don't think so. Didn't you say you wanted
to be a journalist yourself when we met at the coffee
urn last week? You will surely be joining the
meetings in a reporting capacity in no time flat. I
can tell that you are not a woman who shifts from
her goals," Mr. Grant said. Peggy looked to see if
he was poking fun at her again, but she saw that he
was in earnest. She was so tempted to ask him
about the look he had had when speaking to her
about his appointment at The Tribune but thought
better of it.

They did not know each other well enough for
such personal questions, and she could hear Mrs.
Brennan in her head saying "Margaret Anne, you
mind your manners. Nobody wants to have their
lives pried into by strangers. Or friends for that
matter!" Her mother was constantly haranguing her
for her love of watching people and inquiring. But
she knew that the exact reasons that she was
considered impolite by her mother were the
reasons that she would be a wonderful journalist.
She was observant and inquisitive and did not allow
people to stop her. She was startled that he had
remembered their conversation at the coffee urn.
She wondered if that meant that he had thought
about her in his quiet spare moments, as she
thought of him. The thought made her cheeks

warm again, and she felt tongue-tied. She tried to think of something to say, that would not be awkward, but luckily, she was saved by Emily and Eliza emerging from behind the heavy, green velvet drapes again. Em was a sight. The dress fit her perfectly, hugging her curves and flattering her shoulders, which Peggy had always felt were some of her best features. The slit was revealing, without being improper. She looked like Marlo Thomas, headed to a fancy awards banquet with her father.

"Oh, Em! Emily, you look like a million bucks!" Peggy breathed.

"It does fit well, doesn't it?" Emily was back in front of the three-way mirror, appraising herself again, as Peggy had seen her grandfather do when deciding upon which horse to place a bet. Peggy shook her head.

"Emily Monroe, it does not just fit well, it is gorgeous! I really think this is the one Teddy would pick if he were here," said Peggy with conviction. Eliza approached Emily from behind and started to fuss with Emily's hair and the two women were discussing how best the style her hair and what sort of shoes should be worn and just what the men would say when they saw her arrive for cocktails looking like Eliza Doolittle at the ball.

A little while later, Eliza returned with a large white box, imprinted with Bloomingdale's across the lid, a smaller, paper carrier bag containing the silver

strappy sandals they had selected and with a quick
signature to Teddy's account, they parted ways.
Eliza and Mr. Grant, arm in arm, walking across to
the street, undoubtedly, to have the very same
Manhattans that Peggy had had on her mind earlier.
Peggy glanced away from the couple and began
walking to the train station with Emily, heading
home.

The phone rang in the hall. Peggy ignored it, not because it wasn't likely to be for her, but rather because she was engrossed in her Flannery O'Connor short story. Peggy hated to put it down, and adored any book, but especially those written by intelligent women. She was keen to follow the story until the end and did not have any desire to climb out of her warm little nest of Afghan and cushions to cross the floor and out into the cold hallway to answer it. She barely heard the ruckus outside her door as two of her housemates giggled wildly, fighting for the phone. She sipped her coffee and wiped absently at her brown mohair sweater when some of the hot liquid sloshed out of her bottle green milk glass mug. Her mother would have instantly dealt with the sweater, back home, but Peggy had a laxer frame of mind when it came to tidiness. While engrossed in a book, she never thought about the fact that she would be angry with herself when she went to wear the sweater the next time and she saw the faint brown stain, darkening the already brown softness. She tended to allow herself absent-mindedness, but then regretted it, as her mother always warned her that she would. She knew there was a reason that her mother always stressed the need to "care for our things, Peggy dear." Her mother had warned her that when she was paying for her own things, out of her husband's budget, she would be less reckless. And yet, here she was, with very little money to her name, working to save her own money, while she made a name for herself in the newspaper business, and carelessly allowing a $15 sweater to become ruined, as she simply had to know the exploits of O'Connor's Julian. Unfortunately, there was a quick knock and then her door swung open.

"Peg! The phone is for you. It's a man," Rita said, with significant emphasis on the last word.

Rita was always interested in who was speaking to whom, and when and for how long. The fact that a man was calling the house meant that there would be gossip until she could speak to Peggy after the call. Peggy reluctantly placed her ribbon bookmark and shut the book. Getting to her feet, she walked into the hall, took the old black receiver from Rita, and began unwinding the cord to bring it into her room. If she pulled the cord just so she could reach the phone under her bedroom door, and sit on the rag rug carpet, leaning her back against her bed. It was the only way she could get any privacy for a call in this house.

She was lucky to have the room closest to the telephone table, as most of the other girls had to take their calls in the living room, the kitchen or right out in the hall. Just as she turned to shut the door, she noticed that Rita had settled herself on to her bed with an expectant look on her face. Peggy scowled.

"Please, Rita! Out! I will come to tell you every last word of the conversation with my Dad after I finish speaking to him!" Peggy pressed the receiver into her chest hoping that whoever was on the other end was not hearing this discussion.

With a disapproving look, her friend swung her bright yellow legs over the side of the bed and walked out the door.

"Every single word! And for the record – that ain't your Pops," Rita winked, as she shut the door behind her. Peggy slid to the floor, before bringing the receiver to her ear.

"Hello?"

"Hi, is this Miss Brennan?" The voice was familiar, yet Peggy could not place it. "This is she. May I ask who is calling?"

"John Grant. I am sorry to disappoint that I am not actually your dad." Peggy could hear the amusement in his voice. Why was he calling her at home? How did he get her number?

"Mr. Grant! What can I do for you? Did I forget a task at work? I'm afraid I wasn't aware that I had any of your pieces. Do assignment editors do pieces? No, of course, you don't! I'm sorry. I'm rambling... What were you calling for?" Peggy felt flustered. She still could not grasp why her sense seemed to escape her when he was nearby. She prided herself on her composure, among other things, but where John Grant was concerned, she had absolutely no composure whatsoever.

"Please, call me John. No, you did not forget anything at work, although it is work that I wished to speak to you about. Would you be free to meet me tomorrow evening for drinks? I feel that this would be best discussed in person."

"John. Alright, if that's your preference. Tomorrow evening is Saturday. Do you want to talk business on a Saturday night? Won't Eliza be upset?" Peggy cringed as soon as the words left her lips. He was a superior at work, and she had absolutely no business wondering whether his girlfriend would be bothered by his plans for the weekend.

"Eliza? No, I don't think she would be bothered. She doesn't work at The Tribune, so I can't imagine why she would want to join us for a business discussion. Do you happen to have any of your writing? A portfolio of sorts that you could bring with you tomorrow evening?"

"Yes, of course," Peggy's heart leaped. She had not even had to do what Mr. Olson had warned her not to; Mr. Grant, or rather John, had approached her, of his own volition. It did not occur to her to wonder why the Assignment Editor, with whom she had never worked, nor discussed her work in more than just a passing situation wanted to meet her for drinks to discuss her portfolio. "Where and at what time would you like to meet?"

"Do you know the Sudbury?"

"Yes, of course," Peggy answered eagerly, although she had no idea where the Sudbury was. "Alright, let's say the Sudbury, at eight o'clock? I'll meet you there if that's alright."

"Yes, of course," Peggy realized she sounded like a broken record. "Thank you, Miss Brennan. Until tomorrow."

After the line disconnected, Peggy realized that she may have committed an etiquette error by not reciprocating that John could refer to her by her first name as well, but she was too excited by the prospect that her dream was one day from coming true. She was one day from becoming a journalist, she could feel it. Then her office, then her own column, then a Pulitzer. She shrieked and jumped to her feet, and ran to return the receiver to its old, chipped cradle.

"Ritaaaaaaa!!!!!" Peggy shouted to her friend. This was one telephone call that she could simply not wait to repeat word for word.

13

Saturday morning, freshly showered, her hair in curlers, Peggy was sorting through her closet, while the girls were perched all over her tiny room. Peggy had asked about the Sudbury, and upon learning that it was the swankiest restaurant on the East Side, her friends had all rushed to help her pick out an outfit that would be fitting. Something that looked professional, but also fit in with the ambiance. Peggy wanted to look like Elizabeth Montgomery meets Rosalind Russell in His Gal Friday. Emily was also in hot rollers, and her dressing gown, as she had her date with Mrs. Laurel that night. They had all teased her that she had no interest whatsoever in Teddy tonight, just in making a good impression on Mrs. Laurel. Emily had shrugged and said, "and what of it?" The girls had all laughed uproariously at her candor. Mary was sitting propped against Peggy's pillows, her cherubic face framed by her shining curls. She was laying out the collected bottles of nail varnish from each of the women's makeup cases, sorting them by colour, and sorting Rita's contributions into their own Technicolor row, with the fuchsia, acid green, lemon, dark purples and hot pinks making way for the more muted pinks and reds of the others.

"I've never seen white polish before," said Audrey, who was languishing at the end of the bed, her long legs draped nearly to the floor. She held the little glass bottle to the light and turned it in her hand. "It reminds me of type corrector. Rita, where on Earth do you find these things?"

"Oh honey, I just know all the right place to shop! I don't go buyin' all mah things at the beauty counter, ya know," Rita exclaimed with a wink. She was looking through Peggy's delicates drawer, looking for stockings. "Ain't you got nothin' but solid tights, Peggy Sue? You need some patterns and textures in this drawer. I think I'll go take a look and see what I've got that I can lend you." She walked out of the door with a purpose to her step. Peggy wasn't sure that patterned or textured tights were particularly business-like, but on the other hand, she did want to appear modern and in touch.

She reached into the back of her closet and pulled out a black silk New Look dress that had been her mother's when she was younger. It had a fitted bodice, which crossed at the bosom, and a wide skirt that flared from the waist, using yards and yards more fabric than was strictly necessary. It had been cared for so well that though the style was old, the finish of the dress was still immaculate. She held it to herself and turned to face her friends.

"Try it on," said Kate, excitedly. Kate was one of the loveliest girls that Peggy knew, but was not often involved in the activities of the other girls, as she worked as a nanny to a wealthy family uptown, and though she did not live with them, most weeks, it felt that she did, as the parents relied on her to raise their children more than anyone Peggy had ever known. They rarely returned home for the evening before ten o'clock at night, and Kate was expected at work by eight o'clock the next morning. Kate said she truly didn't mind because the boys were simply darling, and that they needed a constant presence in their lives. Peggy thought it sounded dreadful, minding children all those hours, six days a week, but kept that opinion to herself, as she was certain she did not have to restate her disdain for all things domestic. Kate was kneeling on the window seat, her straight blonde hair falling down her back, her cotton blouse tucked neatly into her denim jeans, her elbows balanced on her knees, propping up her strong chin, next to Emily, in her dressing gown and curlers. Peggy felt so pleased and grateful for the women in the room. Her group of love and support.

She slipped the dress on, and zipped up the side, turning to inspect herself in the mirror. It fit like a glove. She stood tiptoe on her bare feet, with her hot rollers covering her head, and put her hands to her waist. She liked her reflection, she liked her figure, she liked her slim pale legs, she even liked the freckles down her thin arms. The women in her room all agreed that this dress, paired with a short, boxy tweed jacket, belonging to Emily, a pair of Rita's black lace textured tights, and Peggy's red patent leather Mary Jane heels would be both charming and winning when it came to her evening. Mary painted her nails the exact cherry red that matched her shoes and then painted Emily's a platinum metallic colour, to offset her sequin gown. Audrey brushed out Peggy's hair and attempted to tame it into a sleek wave, but as usual, it proved impossible, and eventually gather the thick hair into a ponytail at the crown of her head and wound a section around the elastic, for a more sophisticated look. The tiny room soon felt heavy with Aqua Net as Audrey attempted to control the wisps that worked to spring up over Peggy's head.

"I think I'm a lost cause, Audie. My hair is just like me – not quite willing to cooperate," said Peggy somewhat ruefully.

"Well, I give up. I think that's the best we can do at this point. Let's just hope it doesn't start to snow, and mess up all the hard work," said Audrey, tossing the aerosol can and comb onto the bed.

"Well, darlin', if you ain't just the grooviest lookin' thing tonight, and if he don't just drop dead, he's nuts," said Rita, with a wink.

"Rita! I don't want him to drop dead, I want him to take me seriously as a professional and give me an assignment. I am trying to show him that I am a professional and a journalist and that I have talent, and... you know... that I'm..." Peggy trailed off, catching sight of herself in the glass. She smoothed her hand over her hair, took in her delicate cat-eye makeup, her lacquered red lips, and nails, and thought that she did look quite beautiful. While her interests in John Grant were purely professional, she couldn't see the harm in looking as close to stunning as she could get. The pretty girls tended to get noticed at work, so perhaps she could still be a product of the Women's Movement and look dishy. After all, Gloria Steinem was hardly anything to sneeze at, and no one could say she was anti-feminist because of it.

"A professional?" inserted Mary helpfully, with a cheeky smile.

"Hmm? Oh, yes! Exactly!" nodded Peggy. "Thank you for your help, girls. You really are the most."

14

Peggy had intended to take the train to the Sudbury, as her finances did not leave much room for luxury, but as the evening wore on, and the snow began to fall, she worried that the dainty patent leather shoes would be destroyed if she stepped into a snowbank and decided to splurge on a taxi to the restaurant. She attempted to stuff her tiny red, hand-beaded clutch purse with her money, her lipstick, her journal, her tiny pen, and extra pen, her mints, some extra bobby pins, a tiny comb, and some aspirins, and simply could not make the tiny gold clasp catch. She dumped the contents back onto her bed and attempted to rearrange them, and each time, she simply could not make all her 'necessities' fit in this ridiculously tiny purse. She decided to see if any of the items could be placed in her portfolio but then had a vision of John opening the portfolio and having her lipstick and extra pantyhose look back at him. She shuddered at the thought and went back to the tiny clutch. With exasperation, she stamped her foot on her floor and flopped down on her bed. Finally, she decided to do without the pantyhose, the extra pen, the comb, and the bobby pins. She managed to clasp the handbag, before going into the hall to dial for a cab.

Seated in the cab, Peggy lit a slim cigarette and looked over at the driver, himself smoking a short wooden pipe. She thought he looked a bit like her grandfather, with his graying mustache, wide, flat nose, dark hair, graying at the temples, with a flat cap on his head. As he puffed on his pipe, she imagined him returning home at the end of his driving shift for the day, shaking off his cap, before placing it on the old hat rack inside his door, hanging his heavy woolen coat, smelling of smoke, sweat and other people just below the cap, and stepping out his worn leather brogues. Peggy could not see his shoes from her perspective, but she was imagining that he must wear brogues, just like her grandfather. She imagined him walking into a warm kitchen, where his small plump wife would be stirring a warm goulash on the stove. Mrs. Taxi Driver would not be a daring cook, like her grandmother, adding pineapple to everything and calling it 'exotic, dear'. Rather, she would cook as they do in the Old Country – meat, potatoes, salt, pepper, gravy – just the way Mr. Taxi Driver likes it. She imagines Mr. Driver kissing his little wife on the head, taking a deep and appreciative sniff of the goulash, before settling himself at the table. Mrs. Driver would bring him a beer and would bustle around with the final dinner preparations while a large, fat cat lay curled under the table, snoring contentedly. Peggy took a long draw on her cigarette and turned her attention from the imaginary homey scene to the buildings they passed as they wound through the snowy city. Here and there, lights were on, and curtains were still drawn open, allowing passersby a fleeting glimpse into the lives within. They reminded Peggy of dolls' houses rather than real homes, populated by inanimate members, frozen forever in whatever pose she witnessed. This one reading the newspaper before the fire, that one pouring gin into a martini glass, those children watching the snowfall with their noses pressed hard to the glass. A diorama of life in the city, more surreal than real, attention paid to every last detail. Peggy tapped the ash into the tiny, enclosed metal tray in the armrest and glanced at the taximeter. She inhaled quickly. Four dollars, for a cab ride across town. She sincerely hoped that Mrs. Driver's goulash was worth the money. She withdrew four singles, and three dimes, as a tip for coming out in the snow to collect her. She was a firm believer in tipping for service, as a journalist never knew where she might find a credible source, and if she made friends with everyone she met, she was sure they would be more likely to help her when the time came. She stepped out into the cold and pulled her woolen scarf tighter around her neck with her gloved hand. She felt her heel sink deep into the soft snow and knew that even the twenty feet from the cab to the Sudbury's steps would be treacherous and that she would have to mince her steps, so as not to fall. In her mind's eye, she saw herself, bedraggled, borrowed nylons torn, heel broke off her most expensive shoes, covered in snow, attempting to gather her pages back into her wet and splayed portfolio. Her eyes searched for clear

pavement, and seeing none, she straightened her
shoulders, gripped her aged leather portfolio, and
took a step. She felt the smooth leather soles of her
shoes glide on ice hidden beneath the blanket of
white, and her heart skip a beat, as it does when one
knows they are about to fall. She willed herself to
take another tentative step and started when she felt
a firm grasp on her right elbow. With a gasp, she
turned to strike the molesting stranger, and inform
him that she would not be manhandled, only to
come face to face with John Grant. His blue eyes
were bright, and he smiled down to her.

"I apologise for the start, Miss Brennan, but you
seemed to be on the verge of making closer
acquaintance with the sidewalk, and I thought I
ought to offer my assistance. May I escort you in?"

Peggy nodded and allowed him to gently but
steadily guide her to the steps. She was both
relieved to have an arm to lean on in the snows and
disappointed that she would be unable to make a
grand entrance. She had hoped to check her outer
things – coat, hat, gloves, and scarf – at the coat
check, and she had envisioned him, sitting at the
bar, anticipating her arrival, with a scotch in one
hand, a cigarette with a fine wisp of smoke rising
from a heavy ashtray, just in front of him. As she
approached, he would set the highball glass on the
cocktail napkin, smile, and rise to greet her,
admiring her poise and elegance, her stylish attire,
and he would know that he had made the right

choice in promoting her to whatever it was she was certain he was about to promote her to. The thought occurred to her, however, that given the slipperiness of the sidewalk, forsaking her grand entrance, for the less than grand entrance that might have occurred should she have slipped on the ice and become a mess was a price worth paying. She forced the thought that she did not know that Mr. Grant intended to promote her out of her mind and focused on maintaining her composure.

Once inside, John handed over his coat to the coat check girl and then stood to the side while Peggy unwound her thick black scarf, removed her sleek black leather gloves with the red buttons and red piping, and unbuttoned her warm swing coat. As soon as she handed the girl her grey fox fur beehive pixie hat, she picked up her portfolio and turned to face him. She nervously fingered the embossed G.B. on the buttery smooth leather. The portfolio had been her father's, and she had inherited it when she went to college. It made her feel braver to think that her father was with her, at least in initials. She hoped that she would have wonderful news to telephone home tomorrow; news that would make her parents understand why she had given up so much to be where she wanted and needed to be in the world. John offered his arm, and Peggy carefully placed her hand on the inside of his left elbow. She could feel the quality of the wool under her fingers, and it was all she could do to stop herself from petting his jacket. He wore a charcoal three-piece suit, with a maroon paisley silk necktie, wider than any that her father wore, but she assumed this must be the latest style. His black wingtip shoes were shining in the candlelight of the restaurant, obviously polished with consistent regularity. Peggy was uncertain as to whether this was due to extreme wealth or due to a fastidious desire to make his shoes last longer.

They found a high table and perched on the barstools. Peggy found herself wishing that they had chosen a booth, or that the stools had backrests. It was tiresome to spend an evening sitting straight in a backless chair four feet off the ground, but Peggy decided to make the best of it.

"May I get you and your young lady something to drink?" the maître d' directed to John. Peggy's lips tightened and her nostrils flared at this very typical, but highly undesired expectation that as a woman, not only did she not have the capacity to order for herself but that she belonged to the man at the table.

"I think it would be best if you asked her yourself," said John, to Peggy's great surprise.

"Of course, sir," said the maître d', without much interest. He turned his imperious gaze to Peggy, and she returned his look with impunity.

"A Manhattan, please," she said firmly.

"And I'll have a scotch, neat, with a glass of water," John said, and then turned his attention to Peggy.

"Thanks for agreeing to see me on a Saturday. I really want to talk shop with you, before we get back to work on Monday morning."

Peggy nodded eagerly and positioned her portfolio on the small round table between them. "It's no trouble at all," she said enthusiastically.

"So, I have an idea for a new feature in the paper, and my dad has given me the go-ahead to explore the costs and potential revenues associated with such a venture. I instantly thought of you, but I need to see some of your work. Being a feisty woman in life does not always translate to the page, and so I needed to be sure before I set my reputation on the line," John reached for her portfolio, asking her

"May I?"

She nodded and he flipped it open and began rifling through the typed pages and stopping to read a piece now and again. Peggy considered what he said. His dad? What did his dad have to do with anything? A new feature and he had thought of her? He wanted to see how she translated to the page. She felt her breath quicken as she imagined chasing down leads, interviewing politicos, and heads of empire. She pictured herself in a sleek tweed suit, with a snap brim hat, banded by chocolate brown leather. She imagined typing on an electric typewriter and having a secretary go and get her coffee. She felt her cheeks flush, anticipating his reaction to her most vital pieces from the college paper.

"These are good," he said, nodding appreciatively. "Rough, but good. You have a voice, just like I had hoped. I think that if we get you trained up to where I could use you, with a bit of practice." He looked at her expectantly. Peggy tried to ignore the wounded feeling in her gut, which appeared when she did not receive the praise she desired or expected. He thought her writing was rough. He thought she needed training. Who did he think he was? She was a good writer. He would be lucky to have her work for him on his special project. She pressed her lips together to avoid letting her temper get the better of her. She took a deep breath through her nose, composed herself, and took a sip of her cocktail, then thought better of it, and slugged the whole drink in one gulp. It burned her nose and her throat, but it was worth the discomfort to see John look at her with a mingling of surprise, and what she hoped was respect. She would prove that she was better than any of the men. She despised that in order to be considered as good as a man, she had to be twice as good, work twice as hard and put in twice as much effort. It did not occur to Peggy that perhaps this was not a maligning of her gender, but rather that she had no experience in writing for a large newspaper and would require some training before she could be considered a journalist. One did not simply move from the typing pool to the masthead overnight. She kicked her red patent shoe against the table gently and looked at John.

"I am not sure I understand what you mean by them being 'rough'. Those were my most impressive pieces from a very storied career on the paper at my college. If one does not receive training while at college, what does one do there?" she spoke hotly and wished her face would not flush so.

"I do not mean to offend, I just meant that you could do with some editing. I don't know of any journalist worth his salt who gets where he needs to be without some training, without some mentoring, and certainly without some practice. If you do not feel like that is something you would like to do, then I will not waste any more of your time, and we can just enjoy a casual drink as coworkers, and carry on," he lifted the scotch to his lips and took a sip of the clear amber liquid.

He did not flinch or appear in the least bit disturbed by what she knew from her father was a strong liquor. She could feel her chance at advancement slipping away from her and realized that her fantasy would come to fruition, but she had to play the game. Her ego did not handle bruising well, but she knew she could not miss this opportunity, and she knew that she could do what he needed her to do.

"Oh, no, Mr. Grant, I absolutely would be interested. In fact, please tell me more about this special project. You said it has something to do with your father?" she asked with false cheer. She glanced around the dining room for a waiter. She wanted to order another drink. This time she would not gulp it down, but she felt that she needed something to do with her hands. She signaled to a cigarette girl, who approached the table with her tray of cigarettes. John purchased a package of Marlboros, and she took a package of Phillip Morris. She asked the cigarette girl to please send over the cocktail waitress. John lit his cigarette and then leaned across the table to light Peggy's. His lighter was a gleaming Zippo with a mountain scene engraved on the front. He flipped it closed and slipped the lighter back into his breast pocket. She apologized for the interruption and asked him to please continue.

"Well, it has to do with my father in so far as everything at the paper has to do with him. It's difficult not to have something to do with him when he owns the paper," John answered with just the slightest wryness to his voice.

She was beginning to suspect that her earlier assumption from their meeting at the coffee urn had not been incorrect. There was something about the paper that did not make John completely content. Peggy wondered if it was the idea of working for his father that bothered him, or if there was something else. Again, she decided to let that thought lie for the time being. She did not want him to feel that she was prying into his personal business.

"Your father owns the paper? I had no idea! That's incredible. It's just that I suppose Grant is not really such an unusual name, after all, and it did not occur to me to connect the dots. I apologise for my obtuseness," Peggy spoke quickly, eager to move the conversation along to more comfortable topics.

She thought she detected a level of relief in John's face when he realized that she was sincere and that she truly had not known his parentage.

"Yes, well, with regards to the project, I am interested in beginning a Ladies' page in the paper. Something that would appeal to women and girls and hopefully bring more readership to the paper. If we broadened our reader base, we could broaden our marketing avenues, and include ads aimed at ladies."

Peggy, ignoring his assertion that women did not read The Tribune in its present state, bit her lip, pulled her lips to one side, then took a puff on her cigarette. She glanced at a couple near the window. They were elderly and seated across from one another. The woman was gently cutting her steak, while the man took a sip of his water. She could picture them in their kitchen at home, sunlight streaming through the window, him at their table, reading the paper over coffee, while she moved around the kitchen preparing his breakfast. She would move much more slowly now than she had as a young bride. Her movements would be deliberate, painstaking. In her brief imagining, Peggy wondered if it was that women like this, or like her sisters or her mother were not interested in the news or if they simply did not have the time to sit and read the paper. What would give them cause to read the news?

"Do you not agree, Mr. Grant, that The Tribune already has articles aimed at women? The Home page features recipes, homemaking tips, and dress patterns. Surely if you must be able to market those pages towards women."

"That's not the type of ladies' page that I want. I am talking about something revolutionary. I'm thinking less Betty Crocker and more Betty Friedan. Interesting things are happening in the world, and there are women like you who would probably be more likely to read the paper if there was actual news about women. I don't mean dress patterns or how to fix your hair for when your husband gets home. I think women want to know about the Women's Movement," John's face flushed with excitement as he discussed his idea, and as an afterthought, he reminded her to please call him John.

Peggy was surprised by his subversive idea. He was

the first man she had ever met who did not think of the Women's Movement as a bunch of silly women who could not find husbands. She was electrified by the thought that The Tribune would be home to such a section. And even more, enlivened to think that John wanted her involved in the project.

"Please, in that case, call me Peggy. John, this is a very thrilling prospect. I would be honoured to participate. What, exactly, would be my role in this?"

"Well, we would be sort of working it out as we go, but to begin with, you would, of course, be acting in a typing capacity. No, before you go getting indignant, hear me out. You have the skills to type, but that would not be your sole role. I simply need to be able to present the most cost-effective proposal to Dad, and having people in dual roles would help that along. So, in addition to typing, you would be doing some copy editing, and research, eventually, once you have your sea legs, I would have you begin to work alongside the journalists assigned to the area, with a plan to have you become one yourself, in short order," he watched her to see if he could read her thoughts.

Peggy's bright green eyes sparkled with excitement, her freckles dotted nose and cheeks were flushed, and she bit the left side of her bottom lip. It was a habit that all the Brennan women had when they were thinking about something that delighted them.

Mrs. Brennan had the added habit of poking the tip of her tongue out the right side of her mouth when she was thinking. Joan and Peggy also did this as girls. Sometimes Peggy caught herself and pretended to be licking her lips, as this seemed less embarrassing to her. She was so determined to be unique that she could not even bear to have any resemblance to the family that came before her. In truth, her mannerisms were strictly her mother, and her ambition came directly from her father.

"Yes. I would be ever so grateful for the opportunity. Who will I be reporting to? I can't imagine I would be working directly with you, at least not to start," she said with a touch of coyness.

"No, certainly not. I will be continuing my role as Assignment Editor, but this shall be my niche project. My corner of The Trib that is just mine. I have not selected the reporters yet; however, I have my short list of who I would like. So, your first order of business will be to create a list of pieces that girls like yourself would read. I want to introduce Susie Homemaker to the world outside the suburbs, but more than that I want to appeal to the New Woman. The woman who is left out of the magazines; the woman who does not dream of diapers and slippers; the woman for whom college is not simply a place to find a handsome young doctor, but rather a place to become the young doctor," he spoke with a ferocity that Peggy had not expected. She was amazed to hear her own thoughts spoken out loud to her, with no sense of derision. His handsome face was lit from within, there was a fire in his eyes, and she was sure it was a reflection of her own spark.

"I would like to make a toast," she said, raising her cocktail to him. He lifted his own tumbler and held it aloft, "to making a difference for women, and to real reporting for women." They clinked glasses and sipped. She gazed at him admiringly across the rim of her glass. Her eyes were bright, and there was a red kiss on her glass where she had sipped. She wasn't one for romantic thoughts, she told herself, but there was something very attractive about a man who wanted to advance the cause of women, and something equally attractive about a tall, smart, handsome man who could and would help her fulfill her goals.

The morning light streamed in, rousing Peggy from her sleep. She lay in the sweet place between sleep and awake, not opening her eyes, allowing the smell of coffee to reach her, and the sounds of Sunday morning to slowly filter through to her brain, not quite willing to let go of the pleasantness of dreaming, but no longer fully in Dreamland. As the sounds became louder, she felt the delicate streams of her dream slip between her fingers and finally dissipate. She rolled onto her back and rubbed her eyes with the heels of her palms. She had always been a stomach sleeper since her father had told her and her sisters a trivial piece of information about swallowing spiders in one's sleep. The three little faces had been horrified, and Peggy determined that if she slept on her stomach, then the spiders could not find her mouth, and therefore, she would not swallow any spiders in her sleep. She lay flat on her back, watching the rainbows dance across her ceiling from the prism that she had hung on her curtain rod over the window. As a child, her mother had read her Pollyanna, and hanging the prism in her window had been her own way of playing the Glad Game. She felt a childish sense of delight was the red and yellow and green patches moved ever so slightly as the prism moved in the draft. She stretched and rather than rising to face the day, she reached for the pad of paper on the small case next to her bed that functioned as a writing desk that she could use in bed. She tossed the pad of paper on to the bed next to her, and the riffled around for a pen on her nightstand. She rolled onto her side, stuck the pen between her teeth and reviewed the list she had written before falling asleep. She and John had stayed at the Sudbury until closing, discussing every aspect of the new venture. It had been exhilarating. It had taken her a while before sleep had finally taken her once she climbed into her little bed, so she had begun her list of pieces that John had requested. She scrutinized in the harsh light of morning that perhaps some of the ideas were a bit fanciful and eliminated those that she could no longer remember what the point had been she had been trying to make. She felt last night's excitement begin to bubble up again. She would have stayed in bed all morning, had her stomach not begun to give in to the smell of breakfast wafting from the kitchen, complaining loudly that the salty, unctuous scent of bacon was calling to it. She tossed the list aside, shoved her feet into the well-worn, formerly pink slippers beside her bed, grabbed her fuzzy housecoat from its home at the end of the bed and shuffled to the dining room.

A collection of women were gathered around the dining room table, helping themselves to coffee, tea, and orange juice. Those who had had late nights were decidedly more bedraggled than those who had gone to bed at a decent time. Mary and Kate were both washed and dressed; Kate finishing the last few sips of her coffee before heading off to take "her boys" to the Museum for the day; Mary, folding her napkin neatly beside her plate before walking to church. Every Sunday, Mary would fasten her smart power blue Sunday hat to her blonde curls, don white lace gloves, in spring and summer, or pale-yellow leather gloves in winter, place her tiny prayer book into her matching white or yellow purse and walk around the block to the enormous Episcopal Church for the Sunday Service. Peggy felt that one of her greatest pleasures of living on her own wan no longer following Mother, George, Joan, Linda, Daddy, and Harry down the long center aisle to the Brennan family pew in the Methodist Church. She loathed sitting for what felt like an age on the hard wooden pew, trying not to giggle as Harry made extravagant faces at the Reverend Atticus, as he delivered his solemn address. Harry was "such a boy", her mother would say and tell Peggy that she ought to have more influence on her younger brother, rather than encouraging him to carry on. Peggy felt that it ought to be up to Mrs. Brennan to discipline her son in church if it was so important. Peggy poured herself a steaming cup of coffee from the silver urn in front of her and then noticed a letter, addressed to her sitting on her napkin. She recognized the fine, looping hand as her sister Linda's. She thought it

unusual that Lindy would have written a letter
rather than simply calling, but perhaps she got
bored, sitting around her empty house all day while
her husband was at work.

Maybe letter writing was back in fashion amongst
the housewifery set. She slid the letter into her
pocket, to read at leisure after breakfast, and
poured some cream into her blue China cup of
coffee.

16

Dearest Daisy,

No doubt Mom will have called to tell you about the news by the time this reaches you, but in the event that she hasn't, I need to tell you that I have left Tom. I know that Mother and Daddy, and Joanie and the boys won't understand, but I hope that you will. You have always been the free spirit of the family and have always known you were meant for more. Although you are the youngest of us girls, I have always looked up to you for knowing what you wanted, for going after it, and for never letting fear of disappointing our parents or anyone else get in your way.

I guess I should begin at the beginning... I have been very unhappy in my life for as long as I could remember only, I did not know it. I just thought that the general sense of ennui was part and parcel of life as a woman. But now I am not so sure. Tom doesn't love me; I am sure of it. He spends all of his time at work, and when he isn't at work, he is with his friend Fred. I began to feel like the third wheel in my own home. Fred comes and stays, and Tom takes his part and says that he has no place else to stay and that Fred is his pal, and he can't send him out into the street. I just couldn't bear it anymore. You'd think that Tom and Fred were married, and I was the bothersome visitor. Anyway, that's off topic – I asked Tom to see if Fred could find somewhere else to stay for a while, and he refused. He said that if Fred went, he went. My heart broke. I met a woman in my neighbourhood, and we fell to talking and she made me see that I did not have to be unhappy. I did not have to play second fiddle, and that what did I know about life anyway? I had married Old Tom right after high school. Neither of us had had any chance to spread our wings or to breathe. After talking with her, I began to see that I didn't have to stay in Chicago. There is nothing fastening me to this life. We have no children. (In fact, I hope you don't find this too bold, but Tom has not so much as kissed me since our first wedding anniversary. I don't even remember what it feels like after all this time!!! Please do not share that with Mom!!)

So, Helen (that's the woman I mentioned) and I are moving west! We have packed up her old convertible, and we are heading for San Francisco. It's the start of something new out there. Women are free, and that's what I need. I need to be free. I don't think Tom'll chase me down. After all, he has Fred to keep him company. I wrote to Mother and Dad to let them know that they will not be able to get in touch with me at my old address. I am writing to you from a motor inn in Arizona. I can't believe I am writing these words. I never thought I'd get to see so much of the country, but Helen and I are hitting all the sites on our way. We're not coming back to Chicago, so we won't get the chance to see them again. Although, who knows? Maybe one day we will come back the other way. This nomadic existence is appealing to me, so maybe I will travel the country, back and forth. Maybe I will settle in California.

Maybe I'll move to Paris like Gertrude Stein. I can be anywhere; I can do anything. It's so cathartic. I will write to you again when I am settled in, but I wanted to thank you. Thank you for doing what you needed to do. Thank you for showing me that I could be more than Mrs. Thompson. Thank you for being so deliciously Daisy and opening my eyes to the opportunities. I hope that you are at least as happy as I feel in this moment, drinking cold coffee, and writing you from a rickety Formica topped table, looking over the hot asphalt parking lot into the red Arizona sunset.

All of My Love and a Kiss,

Your Sister

Lindy

17

Peggy dropped the letter into her lap. She picked up her coffee cup and took a sip, then with shaking hands she placed the now chilly coffee back on to the table at her right. She had chosen to open the letter in the quiet sitting room and now wished she had retreated to her bedroom as she usually did. She looked around the room quickly for something wrap around her shoulders, as she was shivering. Feeling icy cold was her typical reaction to shock or stress. It was difficult for her to warm up, and she needed to wrap herself in something warm to think clearly. She spotted an old floral blanket draped over the back of the stiff burgundy sofa near the wall. She picked up the letter, crossed the quaint room in two steps, and flung the blanket around her shoulders in a swift movement. She contemplated nesting on the rigid sofa and decided that she was better off to withdraw to her room. Without a second thought to her cold coffee, or the fact that Anya would be displeased cleaning up after her, Peggy tightened the blanket around her shoulders and bustled up the stairs, almost tripping over the lazy cat that had made the landing his home.

"Rufus! You blasted cat!" she muttered, as he darted through her legs and down the stairs to find a more sensitive soul. She reached her room, and carefully closed the door behind her, before climbing into her bed, and huddling the blankets around her. She brought the letter she was clasping to her face and re-read the opening paragraph. Dearest Daisy. Daisy was Linda's special pet name for Peggy since they were small and had read Little Women together.

When Meg named her daughter Margaret and called her Daisy, Linda had christened her 3 years younger sister Daisy, and to this day it stuck. Even her signature "All of my love and a kiss" came from the Louisa May Alcott classic. Peggy and Linda had read their childhood copy so often between the two of them that Little Women had almost become their secret language, quoting it to each other when they did not want their siblings to understand a thought that passed between them. Peggy worried that Linda had been rash in leaving her marriage with a woman she barely knew and worried that she would regret her decision when it was too late. She could just imagine how Mama and Joanie would be having kittens over this news.

The Brennans had thought Peggy was wild for moving to pursue her dream of journalism and she had not been married, and there was no one to be hurt by her choices. On the other hand, Peggy felt a faint glow of pride that her big sister had seen her as a role model and had made a choice for herself for the first time in her life. But was it for herself? Was this what she wanted, or had she been influenced by this... what was her name? Oh, right, Helen... this Helen? It did sound as though she and Tom were having problems, but were they so serious that they could not be worked out? Tom Thompson, Peggy thought, shaking her head. After ten years knowing him, she still could not believe any parents had been ridiculous enough to name their son Tom Thompson. Tom Thompson, Jr. yet. Tom and Linda had never seemed as affectionate as her perpetually pregnant sister Joan and John Michael, but she simply thought Linda was more reserved. Maybe there was more to it. Maybe that was why Lindy and Tom had never had a baby. If he hadn't kissed her in three years, it seemed unlikely that he was doing anything else that would help produce a child. Peggy's thoughts raced to the last time she had seen the erstwhile Mrs. Thompson and her husband. It had been at Claire's baptism in the spring, she was sure. Linda and Tom had returned to their little town for George and Nancy's fourth baby's baptism, as they were to be made godparents. She remembered the pained expression on Lindy's face as she cuddled the bundle of white satin and lace that was her goddaughter.

She had nuzzled her face into Claire's neck and kissed her white capped head. Tom had stood stoically by, appearing to be particularly interested in the rose glass windows of the church, and not particularly interested in the service. At the time, Peggy had thought nothing of it, as she herself found Church services to be dull; now she wondered if it was more to do with the point of the service. Maybe Tom did not like children? Maybe Tom did not like to be with Linda any more than she now liked to be with him? Maybe it was a blessing that no child had been forthcoming. Maybe it was wise if the two of them went their separate ways.

Suddenly, Peggy seized on an instinct. Perhaps it was her inner journalist seeking the truth. Perhaps it was idle curiosity; or perhaps it was simply her love for her older, and closest, sister that caused her to pull the telephone from its perch on the telephone table and settle into her spot on the floor in her room, the line taut under her bedroom door, and begin dialing her sister's phone number. She knew that Linda was not there, but it was not Linda she wanted to speak to at this time. She needed to speak to Tom. Before she spoke to her mother or even Linda, she needed to know if her suspicions were true. The phone was answered on the second ring by a gruff voice, which sounded thick with sleep. Peggy glanced at the clock on her bedside table to confirm that it was almost eleven o'clock in the morning and that she should not be waking her brother-in-law.

"Hullo?"

"Hey, Tom? It's Peggy," she said quickly.

"Uh no, it's not Tom. Let me get him for you," said the gruff voice. There was a dull clang as the receiver was placed on a hard surface, and Peggy could hear the voice shout in a muffled tone for Tom. She heard more rustling, then a click as the phone was picked up, and a second click as the initial receiver was placed in the cradle.

"Hello?" said Tom, quietly.

"Hi, Tom, it's Peggy. I'm sorry to disturb you if you have company. I wanted to talk to you about Linda."

"Oh," said Tom, and then after a pause, "well, that isn't company. That's Fred. He's kinda liked a roommate, I guess you might say. And as for your sister, I got no idea where she is. She just kinda made off with that friend of hers, and I haven't heard from her in a week, so I don't have much to tell you about that." She heard a tightening in his voice, and she imagined him sitting at the breakfast bar in the apartment that he had shared with Linda, wrapping the cord around his fingers and then loosening it again, as he tried to anticipate what she would say. Tom was a tall, bulky man, who still had the frame of the high school football player he had been five years ago.

"I see. So, Linda left, and yet Fred is still there. I got a letter from Lindy, and she seemed to feel that Fred was a basis for the problems that caused her to leave..." Peggy let her voice trail off, waiting from Tom's reply. He scoffed on the other end of the line.

"Listen, Peggy, I appreciate your concern, but our problems are none of your business. Fred is not, nor has he ever been the problem between your sister and me. I'll thank you to keep your nose out of other people's business. And maybe mention that to your family before the entire Brennan brigade marches up to my door. I don't need the hassle." At that, Peggy heard a click and then the signal indicating that Tom had disengaged. She sat clutching the telephone receiver to her chest for a moment, unsure what to think. She had assumed that she could glean more information from her brother-in-law, but instead, she was surprised to find that he was still chumming with the reason Linda had left, going so far as to refer to him as a roommate. She slowly lowered the heavy old receiver back to the cradle, engaging the plunger. She reached over her head, behind her onto her bed, blindly groping for the letter, before picking up the phone to dial home. She listened to the crackly line ringing across hundreds of miles and hoped desperately that Harry would be home and would be the one to pick up.

"'Lo?" Peggy smiled as her younger brother answered the phone.

"Well! What happened to 'Hello, Brennan Residence'?" she couldn't help ribbing her brother.

"Hey Peg. Nah, I don't wanna sound like a square if people call. I have been getting calls from Barbara lately, and I want her to think I'm some sorta nerd," Harry said with sincerity.

Peggy smiled, Harry was only a year younger than her, and still lived at home, with no aspirations for college, while working at the filling station just outside of town. Peggy knew her mother was in no rush to have her youngest fly the nest and would be happy to have Harry stay at home for as long as possible.

"Barbara, hey? Barbara Campbell?" Peggy asked, with curiosity.

"No, not Barbara Campbell, Barbara Kidd. She's new since you moved. Her folks just moved to town, they opened a grocery store on Main, and she's a sophomore at Newton. You'd like her. She's a groovy chick."

"She's a chicken?"

"Peg! You know what I mean. She's a fox."

"Well, which is it? A chicken or a fox? They're hardly similar animals," Peggy loved to tease her little brother, and she despised hearing women referred to as animals.

"Ugh, why you gotta be so difficult? How 'bout this –Miss Kidd is a fine, upstanding young woman, and I feel strongly that you and she are gonna get along great," Harry adopted his version of a fancy accent, playing back to his sister.

"I cannot wait to meet her. If you love her, I'll love her," Peggy smiled.

"Whoa, whoa, whoa! Hold your horses, Margaret! Who said anything about love? I just said she's been calling and she's great, we ain't nowhere near love," Harry said quickly. Yet Peggy silently added to herself.

"Alright, alright. I won't put the cart before the horse. Hey, I need to get some homeward info, and I don't want to ask Mom or Daddy. Have you heard anything about Linda lately?"

"Have I? Holy Mackerel, that's all I been hearing lately. Mom and Pops are practically losing their minds over here. Mom's cryin' that she's never gonna have grandchildren. Pops' reminding her that she already has Joan's, and Georgie's kids, and ain't hurtin' for babies to kiss. Pops' is convinced that Tom has done somethin' to her that made her run off. Mom's saying that it's because they don't got kids and that a woman can never be real happy without kids. It's like living in Bizarro over here. I never 'spected this of Lindy, to be honest. This is more your gig. Lindy and Joanie are so much more... I dunno... conventional, I guess. At least that's what I thought. Mom is saying that the girl she run off with musta kidnapped her or brainwashed her. She says that only hippies and cultists go to San Francisco. I swear, she has half a mind to fly to

California, and drag her back home to her husband," Harry lost all tone that he was kidding around. Peggy could tell that he was serious and that things at home had been a challenge. She could just picture Mrs. Brennan, in her black woolen coat, sensible sturdy black shoes, neatly appointed black hat, with red plastic cherries on the left side, storming off the airplane, through the San Francisco of her imagination, shouting Linda's name, and demanding that she show herself right now, as she had done when they were children and their mother had found a broken vase, and none of the five children would appear, nor would they own up to the fault.

"Wow. Hey, can I tell you something? I want your opinion, but I don't want to say anything to Mama or Dad until you tell me what you think. I feel like I am betraying a confidence, but I think, in a way, that Mama might be right and that there may be something going on in the Thompson house that chased Linda away," Peggy dropped her voice, conspiratorially. She had a sickening feeling that she ought to keep the contents of the letter and of her brief call to Tom private, but she felt she would burst if she didn't tell someone. She knew that in his quiet way, Harry would never betray their sister's wishes.

"Oh?"

"Yeah. So I received a letter this morning from Linda, saying she was in Arizona, with her friend

Helen, and that she was leaving Tom, and that, basically, Tom was putting his friendship with this fellow Fred ahead of his marriage, and that Fred was staying in their house, and that Tom refused to put him out," Peggy said quickly, as though saying it all at once would relieve her of the burden.

"She left her husband because of guest who is overstaying his welcome. I dunno. I don't buy it. That seems like a pretty lame excuse to up and take off for the West Coast," said Harry skeptically.

"That's not the half of it! She said that Tom hasn't so much as kissed her since their first wedding anniversary! Can you believe it? And when I called their house to talk to Tom, Fred answered the phone, and then Tom said Fred isn't company and that he is more of a roommate. What do you make of that? And it doesn't seem to me that Tom has any interest in hunting down our sister. Almost like he's relieved that she's gone," Peggy said breathlessly. She told herself that this was not gossip and that as Harry was both of their brother, he should know what was happening. She had the smug satisfaction of a woman who truly believed that they were doing the right thing, although no one had asked her to become involved, and all parties may have preferred that she allow them to do what they felt was right.

"Huh. That's not... great. I wonder why that guy is still living there. He and Tom must be really

close, or that guy really knows how to wear out
his welcome," Harry spoke haltingly.

"Do you think that there is a chance that maybe Tom
doesn't love our sister?"

"I guess so. I can't imagine not kissin' your wife in 4
years if you loved her and she was right there."

"I think that Tom is having an affair and having that
Fred there is the excuse he used to not have to be...
ummm... intimate with Linda! Maybe he has a
mistress!" Peggy blurted her suspicion to her
brother.

"Well, I know a lotta guys do that, but mosta them
don't move their buddy into their house to cover
their tracks. Maybe those two things don't go
together? Maybe he's having an affair, and his
buddy is annoying? I dunno. Sorta makes sense to
me, when you put it that way," Harry mused.

Peggy pictured her brother running his fingers
absently through the dark forelock that refused to
stay out of his eyes. One thing that all the Brennan
children had in common was their incorrigible hair.
Mrs. Brennan spent hours working to smooth and
flatten and curl and straighten and generally tame
the hair on each of her children's heads, but
usually, in the time it took to work from oldest to
youngest, the first head would have become
disheveled before she had finished. Peggy had been
around ten years old when Mrs. Brennan had
finally given up, bought a bottle of spray and a tube

of Brylcreem for the boys and left them to the wills of fate. When Harry was thinking, he would absently tug at his forelock, or finger brush it back over his head. Many a dinner table conversation would be interrupted by a sharp "Henry Fitzgerald Brennan! Stop fussing with your hair! Do you want to get it in your food?" Often Harry would look up at their mother, almost as though he had just now realized, he was in the room with others.

"Well, I don't know nothing," Peggy stifled her urge to correct her younger brother's grammar. "I'm just thinkin' that maybe it ain't no mistress. Maybe him and the fellow..."

It dawned on Peggy that her brother was

implying something different than a

mistress. "Harry, you can't mean... but

that's not even legal! You can't mean it,

surely!"

"Well, I dunno, but it is legal in Illinois. Been legal thereabouts since '62. Last I heard, Chicago is in Illinois. And if I am remembering, Lindy and Tom got hitched and moved there in '61. So, he'd know it, too."

"Oh gosh, Harry. Is that so? I did not know this. How did I not know??" Peggy was both distressed, and slightly offended that her brother, whom she considered to be less intelligent and certainly less worldly than herself would know a piece of cultural and social information that she did not.

"Well, gosh, Peg," Harry adopted her hysterical tone, in a teasing manner, "I just can't rightly say! I mean, you were all of 17 in 1961, and busy trying to get yourself graduated and off to college. I imagine the state of affairs three states over wasn't high on your list of things to think about."

"Harry!" Peggy exclaimed in a frustrated tone used by sisters the world over when they feel they are being mocked by Baby Brother. "I must think. We need to find out. We need to fix this. We need to investigate." Peggy was picturing herself sitting across a sleek oak desk from a man in suspenders, his shirtsleeves rolled up, smoking a cigar, while she tearfully handed him a photograph of Tom and Linda on their wedding day, and begged him to help her find her sister, so they could put their family back together. In her fantasy, she wore a sleek black dress, her imaginary blonde hair piled in becoming tendrils and smoked from a long cigarette holder. Just as she began musing whether she should consider bleaching her hair, she heard Harry speak.

"Why?" he simply stated.

Confused at being pulled from a reverie, she wondered why he would question her choice to bleach her hair.

"Why what?" she asked.

"Why do we 'have to' do anything? Why do we have to get involved? If Linda had wanted us to get involved, she would have come to us, instead of high tailing it across the country. If Tom is having an affair with a woman, that's terrible, and he oughtn't do that to his poor wife, and if he is queer and this
Unless..." Harry trailed off.
Peggy's ears pricked. "Unless what? What do you know, Harry?"
Fred fellow is his... I dunno... whatever it is that you call it, what does it matter to you? This is their life, Peg. If Lindy is happy traveling and seeing the coast, then good for her. If Tom is in love with Fred, that's fine too. His wife left him, he lives in a State where nobody don't give two hoots what he does, and it is none of your damn business!"

Peggy held the phone away from her ear and stared at it, as though the face of the receiver may give her clues into this sudden liberal, sure of himself brother of hers.

"But..." Harry interrupted her. "No buts, but nothin'. You mind your own. You worry about your life. You worry about getting' that byline. Don't go meddlin' where you ain't wanted." As strange as it felt, Peggy could see that her brother had a point. Lindy had said she was happy and free for the first time in years. And if Tom and Linda were no longer married, it really did not matter to her what Tom chose to do, because Linda chose to leave him.

"Ok, Harry, ok. You're right."

"Sorry? Say that again?"

"I said you're right; I have to mind my own business."

"Say what? I think we've got a bad connection. Say it again. Just one more time."

"I SAID YOU'RE RIGHT!!" Peggy shouted clearly. Anya poked her head around the corner in concern at the commotion. Peggy smiled and waved her away.

"Yeah, I know, I just had to hear you say it again. And then again." Harry exploded into a loud guffaw that made Peggy smile.

"Oh, you!!!" she smiled to herself, enjoying this moment of fraternal teasing and affection. AS much as she adored the solitary life, she was creating for herself, chasing her dream, she missed the easy tenderness that is home. Even the small annoyances she thought of with fondness, as she no longer fought with her sisters over the bathroom, or worried that George would tell his cute friend that she hated sports when she was trying to finagle a date to the homecoming game. Along with the frustrations, her family had been a haven. A place where Mama smoothed her covers as she drifted to sleep, where Dad handed her a book that he had finished and thought she would enjoy, where she and her sisters would giggle uncontrollably after the lights were turned out, where George would pick her up from a sleepover in the middle of the night when she and a friend began to argue too much. The transition from childhood to adulthood was more wistful than she had expected it to be. She had expected to move on in her life, chasing her star, knowing her family was behind her but not looking back because what was coming was so amazing. Now, she found that she did look back. She had always known she did not want to be a housewife with kids and no option for a career. She wanted to do interesting things, and see interesting things, and be interesting. She had always assumed that she had to have one exclusive to the other. She wondered if it might be possible to have the haven of a home, and the cut glass ashtray with the park out her corner office window.

"Thanks, Harry. I am glad we got to talk it out. Call me if you need me. Or better yet, come visit! If Mother and Dad start driving you nuts, I can show the tallest building you have ever seen and take you for a cocktail in a fancy bar." She smiled, picturing Harry in his plaid button-down shirt and dungarees in a cocktail bar.

"Ha! How about a beer and a dog? That's more my speed, Peg. I'll see if I can get a day off at the garage and come up and see ya."

"Sounds like a plan, maybe bring the delightful Miss Kidd with you. I've never met a chicken that was also a fox. Brings whole new meaning to the fox is in the hen house," Peggy laughed loudly at her own joke.

She often found herself much funnier than anyone else seemed to. She often felt it was a shame that others could not appreciate what she saw as a discerning sense of humour.

"Ha! That'll be the day. I gotta go, sis. Talk to you soon?"

"Definitely. Thanks, little brother." Peggy placed the receiver into the cradle and dropped her head back against the side of her bed. She gently fingered the tatty quilt that she had taken from the sitting room. The cotton was so thin in places, and the fill had clumped in the edges, leaving diaphanous sections that were little more than two layers of sheeting. She rubbed her neck with her right hand, causing red marks to appear on her nearly translucent skin, a nervous habit that she had developed when she was a girl.

18

The ancient typewriter clunked loudly as Peggy typed up another dreary piece written by Mr. Olson. She was intent on her work and did not notice when John approached her desk and stood next to her. The typing pool was generally a deafening space, with the typists and typewriters talking and banging away. Sarah telling Hannah and Susan about her mother's health; Angela and Caroline discussing their dates by the coffee urn; women groaning in frustration when their keys became stuck or ran out of correcting fluid. When Peggy first arrived at The Tribune, she had some difficulty adapting to the noise, as she was used to the quiet of the library and study hall at her small college. She did not know how she would be able to concentrate in such a distractingly loud space; over time, she came to realize that there was not much need to concentrate, per se, when simply typing other men's work. She simply made sense of the chicken scratch and typed what she read. She learned to zone into her work and thereby spent most of her working day in her own little world, as Mrs. Brennan described it many times over her life.

"Miss Brennan?" John said finally when he realized that Peggy would not be looking up from her work in the near future. He saw her brow furrow, as she peeled her eyes from the foolscap from whence, she had been typing.

"Hmmm?" said Peggy, as she looked up. "Oh! Mr. Grant. I'm sorry, I didn't see you there! What can I do for you?" Peggy smiled sweetly, imagining herself to be adorably attentive, in her face and demeanor.

"I noticed that" John chuckled, "I need to borrow you for the next couple of hours. I have cleared it with Mr. Latham, so if you wouldn't mind finishing what you are doing, and then joining me in my office?"

"Of course, not a problem," she glanced quickly back to her document, "give me a quarter of an hour and I will be happy to join you." Peggy smiled again, then realized that she had been familiar with her superior, and added quickly, "please. If that works for you."

"That is fine, thank you. Please bring your notepad and a pen." He gave her a quick smile, before he turned on his heel, and headed toward Mrs. Kelly's desk. Mrs. Kelly was an elderly woman, in Peggy's eyes, but in truth, she was only fifty years old, and in perfect physical health. Mrs. Kelly supervised the women in the typing pool while answering phone calls and directing the pageboys. Peggy wondered what John thought a dinosaur like Mrs. Kelly could offer his new column. With her russet hair streaked with grey, her cat eyeglasses, boxy suit dresses, and equally boxy pumps, Peggy was certain that Mrs.

Kelly was no more 'with it' than her own mother. With a scrunch of her delicate nose, Peggy opened the tight top drawer of her desk, and withdrew her powder compact and lipstick tube, and headed quickly for the ladies' room, leaving her cigarette in the ashtray, still pluming a delicate strand of smoke, her paper still in the typewriter, midsentence, and her chair messily untucked from her desk.

Peggy frowned at her reflection in the dingy old mirror over the heavy porcelain sink. The bottom right corner of the mirror was smoky from decades of steam peeling at the mirror backing. Peggy smoothed her hands over the front of her hair, willing the unruly strands to lay flat. She pursed her lips and exhaled through her nose in aggravation as the errant hairs continued to pop in all directions, as soon as she removed her hands. She opened her compact and tapped the excess powder on the edge of the sink, before dabbing at her nose and forehead with the translucent dust. After she snapped the lid shut, she spun up her lipstick and applied the rusty red to her lips, smacking her lips together, and then sucking her index finger, as Joanie had taught her when she was 10, to ensure that no colour landed on her slightly crooked front teeth. Peggy washed her hands, smoothed her pencil skirt, adjusted her powder blue acrylic sweater, and gave herself a final appraising look. With the exception of her hair, Peggy thought there was little to be concerned about with regards to her appearance. Her grandmother's pearl and rhinestone brooch glinted in the light from the left shoulder of her sweater, her chignon was the best she could possibly do with her wiry hair, her skirt was becoming to her figure, and her matching blue t-strap suede pumps made her feel that those who looked at her, saw a very put together, young woman. Blowing herself a kiss in the mirror, Peggy headed back to her desk to pick up her purse, with her notebook and pen and make her way to Mr. Grant's office.

Opening the door to John's office, Peggy was surprised to find the room teeming with women. Some young, like her, some older, some on chairs, some leaning against the outer walls, there was even a young woman who had perched herself on the slim window ledge. Peggy thought that it was a good thing it was winter so the young woman did not fall out the window, and also because the office would have been stifling in the summer with these many bodies crammed into one space. Peggy was momentarily distressed. Had John made the same proposal to all these women that he had made to her? Was she not the wunderkind she had thought that he thought she was? Was she meant to share the glory with all these women? Or Peggy thought with panic, was she meant to compete with these women for a position that she had understood to be hers? Peggy flashed with anger, as she remembered Daddy telling her that one must never trust a man in business. A man in business is only ever looking out for himself. He had laughed when she had said that certainly he wasn't like that and that he was a very successful man in business.

"Kitten, the only reason that I am a very successful businessman is that I am only out for myself. To provide the best for your mother and you and your brothers and sisters. If I cared one lick about the other fellows, I would have been eaten up and spat out ages ago." He had pinched her cheek, kissed her curly head and chuckled again.

"There she is!" John slapped his hand on his knee and stood up as Peggy turned her bewildered face towards him and looked around for a place to sit. She was determined to establish herself as a force to be reckoned with, and she was not about to give up her dream office with her cut-glass ashtray easily. "Ladies, allow me to introduce Miss. Brennan. Miss. Brennan is sort of our Gal Friday in this new department, and over the next few days, I think you will find her to be indispensable."

Peggy nodded at the women as they quietly said their hellos, then rounded on John.

"Mr. Grant?" Peggy said through the tightest of smiles and gritted teeth, "May I speak to you in the hall just for a quick moment? I have a rather... personal... issue that I need to discuss with you." She turned and walked back out of his office, with him following closely behind.

"What's wrong? You seem upset," John said, with a confused expression, his left hand never leaving the brass knob on his door. Peggy could hear a murmuring rising through the transom as the women spoke amongst themselves.

"I seem upset, do I? Gee, Mr. Grant, I can't imagine why. Oh, wait! I remember! Because there is a room full of women in your office, which I walked into, without warning that I was walking into a room full of women!" Peggy's green eyes flashed and narrowed; her grip tightened on the pen that she was holding and jabbing the air with emphasis. "What happened to this being a small operation? Just a few of us? If you expect me to compete with those women for a job that was already mine three weeks ago, then you have another think coming, sir!"

"What? Do you think that this is some sort of casting call? I don't know if I've ever heard of an open audition for writers before. I thought that was an acting and modeling thing..." His blue eyes twinkled with amusement. Peggy felt anger bubble anew. She was tired of this man finding her frustrations amusing. She may be from a small town, she may be new to this, but she was determined. She was not a petulant child for his amusement. She had to stop herself from stamping her foot, as she felt that would take away her argument at not being a petulant child and jutted out her chin. She refused to speak, and watched his face, waiting for him to explain. "No, you are not competing for this job. I have rounded up as many women as I could find who was free today, and we will do this again for the next three days, gathering as many women as we can, so that we can find out what women want to read about. This is a... hmmm... a... focus group," he searched for the correct words.

Peggy dropped the hand that had been jabbing the pen in John's direction, relaxed her grip and said with dignity, "Well, I don't see why you couldn't have just told me that! It is not fun to be surprised like that!" Peggy felt better. She felt that the rug was no longer pulled out from beneath her.

"Not a big fan of surprises, eh?" said John thoughtfully.

"No. Not one bit," said Peggy firmly, pursing her freshly painted lips. She felt the familiar smooth, and slightly sticky waxiness as her lips touched of the new lipstick.

"I guess I had better cancel the marching band and cheer squad that I had hired for this afternoon," said John, as he opened the door and hurried back into his office. Peggy rolled her eyes toward the ceiling and followed him into the room.

19

"Well, personally, I think that what you kids are trying to do here is just wonderful! I mean, a whole column in the paper just for us girls. I swear, my mother, well, she was a suffragette you know, and she wrote an entire magazine with her girlfriends at our kitchen table when I was a girl, and I swear she would just be jumping for joy to see me here sitting with a genuine girl reporter working for a big fancy magazine like The Tribune. Golly! It's just swell!" Peggy sat across the narrow table from Miss Annie Millers, a dainty octogenarian, with blued hair pulled into an intricate pattern of swoops and curls and pins, the tiny fingers of her left hand delicately fingering the rim of the jadeite mug holding her orange pekoe tea, her left hand, weighed down by what looked to Peggy like very heavy, very tarnished costume cocktail ring, gesticulated wildly as she emphasised her points. Peggy thought that Miss Millers was tremendously overdressed for the diner that John had brought them to engage in individual discussions with each member of the focus group, before reuniting in the boardroom at the paper and participating in an open discussion with everyone.

"Oh, thank you, Miss Millers. I should mention again, for the purpose of total clarity, that I am not a reporter. Well, not yet anyway, and The Tribune is a newspaper, not a magazine. But I am glad you think your mother would be impressed, and I am glad you are here talking to me," Peggy poised her left hand over the notepad, gripping her pen and trying to steer the conversation back to the questions at hand. So far Miss Millers had taken every opportunity to speak without actually answering the question at hand. "Now, just quickly, that last question again?"

"Oh, certainly!" Miss Millers beamed at Peggy over the pale green mug, "Which question was that dear?" Peggy stifled a frustrated sigh and reminded herself that she must learn to control her temper and her patience if she was ever going to get anywhere as a writer. Journalists who lost their patience lost their scoop.

"Umm... the question was: Would a women's column in the newspaper make you more likely, less likely, or no change as to whether you would continue to subscribe to The Tribune?"

"Oh, you sweet thing you! Well, I'd have to say, firstly, with no offence intended of course, so don't you mind me one second, but firstly, I am not, personally, nor have I ever been a subscriber to The Tribune. I am and always will be a New York Times girl. So, I suppose the answer to that would be no change. I mean, I would certainly be glad if the Times were to start a ladies' column, but it doesn't matter to me in that sense, as you know, I am and always will be a New York Times girl. Now, as I said... no offence intended, as I hope you know that that does not mean for one second that I personally wouldn't be able to offer some great ideas as to what should go into that sort of column. My mother was a suffragette after all."

Miss Millers' thin lips formed a broad smile, and Peggy could see little pink lines where her vibrant lipstick had bled outside of her lip line.

Peggy nodded and wrote Miss Millers' answer in shorthand on her sheet of notepaper. She scanned the diner quickly, to where John was interviewing a beautiful dark-haired young woman, who was pretending to find his questions to be the most intellectually stimulating thoughts she had heard all week, then quickly, to where Mrs. Kelly sat smoking and drinking coffee, while her interview subject meekly filled out her own answers on a sheet of paper, as though she were writing a high school English exam, and finally to Caro Nance, the junior reporter at the paper, whom John had brought in to clinch the team. Peggy was both awed by, and extremely wary of Caro, as Caro was the embodiment of what she wanted in life, or at least close to what she wanted in life, but Peggy was often leery of Caro's changeable nature – sweet and thoughtful one moment and then crackling with energy and annoyance the next. Peggy did not realize that the things that made her wary of Caro were the exact traits that made many give she herself a wide berth. Peggy felt she could learn much from the woman, but knew that if she stepped in Caro's way, it wouldn't take much to be on the receiving end of one of her infamous tongue lashings. Caro was writing feverish notes as she spoke with the woman who had been perched on John's windowsill in the office.

"Well, perhaps after this, you might decide to take in the Times and The Tribune," Peggy said with a perky smile, before reaching for her own, now-tepid, mug of coffee.

She thought of her Dad telling her mother that it was a good idea to take in more than one paper so that a body could learn more than just one newspaper man's opinion on the news. Mr. Brennan felt that the news always took the slant of the man who owned the paper, and insisted, even in their Podunk town, with its one stoplight, that they must take at least three newspapers to "really know what was happening in this big ol' world".

"Oh dear, aren't you just a doll? Well, I may pick up a paper or two, if your name is on it, dear, but personally, I don't think it would do to subscribe to more than one paper anyway. I mean, once you've read it once, it just isn't news anymore, now, is it?" Miss Millers narrowed her eyes, as she made her last point.

Peggy had to admit that that argument was difficult to challenge. Miss Millers sipped daintily at her tea, and Peggy wondered how the woman had come to be in John's office today when she clearly did not feel any love or involvement of or with the paper that they worked for. Had she simply walked in off the street, hoping to find someone to talk to?

"Thank you so much for your time, Miss Millers. If you wouldn't mind, I would like to walk you back to the main table, where you will be comfortable until we return to the office," Peggy rose from her seat, aware that there was little chance of Miss Millers moving away from her if she did not guide her herself.

She stood, and guided Miss Millers, and her 'personally's back to the table where the rest of the women were sipping tea or coffee following their interviews with one of John's groups. Peggy was preparing to ask the next woman to join her at her table when she felt an icy blast of cold air rustle her hair and send a shiver down her spine. A woman, bundled cozily in black fur and wool and leather had entered the diner and was stamping her feet, either to warm them or to dust the snow from them, or perhaps both.

"Jawwwwwwn darling!" cried a familiar voice from amongst the black bundle of fabrics. Peggy glanced sharply and realized that it was Eliza from Bloomingdale's. Peggy rolled her eyes and directed her attention to the list on the table, to determine who was to be interviewed next. She pretended to be oblivious as Eliza crossed the diner and kissed John on his smooth cheek, placing both of her gloved hands on his shoulders. What difference did it make to her if John chose to invite Eliza to their focus group? She hadn't known about it in the first place, so it really made no difference to her. He could bring her any place he chose. She would remain professional. She would not become the woman that she feared she was becoming around him – the jealous, heartsick woman who thought of nothing but a man. She had her life plan, and the plan was to become a successful journalist. Her success was only tied to John Grant insofar as he could help her establish herself at the paper. It was perfectly reasonable to have a working relationship with her boss that was pleasant and courteous. She would not become the silly little woman trope. She saw girls like that all of the time – perfectly capable, sensible women, who were treated like small children should they display any sense of whimsy, and the logical, clucking man would come along, dust them off, and kiss their noses, as though they were little girls who needed Daddy`s guidance. The only fatherly guidance she needed came from her own father, not from a dashing young man who cut a nice figure in his well-cut suits.

"I'll take Elizabeth Lynton, please," said Peggy quickly, looking up from the list, unsure if Elizabeth Lynton was a Miss or a Mrs. She silently cursed Mrs. Kelly for not labeling the list with appropriate prefixes. She hated to be caught unaware.

"That's me, dear!" Peggy looked up at the trilling

voice. Taking a deep breath, Peggy bit her tongue, as her mother had raised her to – "Margaret Anne! If you can't keep a civil tongue, you will bite your tongue!" Of course, Eliza would be short for Elizabeth. Of course, she was there to be interviewed for the column. Of course, that was why she was there. Why wouldn't John Grant want the lovely Eliza's opinion? She was clearly smitten with him, and she could only imagine that he was just as smitten with her.

"Oh, wonderful," said Peggy flatly, "Can I get you a tea or coffee? You must be chilled out in this weather." Peggy glanced at the tree rustling in the boulevard out the large plate glass window facing the street.

"Yes! Thanks! Coffee! Thanks!" Eliza chirped each word with the same wide, lovely smile that Peggy imagined she used with every customer in the dress salon. Peggy signaled to the short flat haired girl at the counter that Eliza would be joining her at the little table in the corner, and to bring the coffee pot.

"Please, join me, Miss Lynton," Peggy indicated to the seat against the wall, intentionally angling herself to block Eliza's view of John's charcoal back, before realizing that this was ludicrous, childish behaviour, and settled herself, without concerning herself with Eliza's line of sight. "Thank you ever so much for coming down."

Eliza slipped off her wool and fur coat and laid

them on the seat next to her, then she carefully placed the black leather gloves on the table next to her flatware. Peggy thought this was a rather silly place to put something you did not wish to spill coffee on but kept her thoughts to herself. Eliza removed the fluffy angora cap and proceeded to puff out her bangs, and then ran her fingers along her eyebrows, as though checking to ensure that they had not become mussed. Peggy, in her infinite curiosity about others, caught that small action and wondered if it was a vanity or a nervous tic that caused it. To Peggy's surprise, Eliza reached her right hand across the table and said "Please, call me Eliza. I do not go by Elizabeth. It sounds so old fashioned." Peggy was startled to hear her own thoughts on her choice of diminutive for her name echoed back to her from this elegant young salesclerk.

"Thank you, Eliza. Please call me Peggy," shaking the young woman's hand, Peggy debated as to whether she should bring up their meeting a few weeks ago at the dress salon at Bloomingdale's, then decided to simply carry on with the conversation, as they had a lot of ground to cover in only a couple of days, and her corner office, with a beautiful window overlooking the park, or the street, or even the air shaft, and the cut glass ashtray were depending on her helping John to establish this women's column.

Peggy pulled her list of questions out from under the jadeite coffee mug and picked up her pen. Just as she was about to ask Eliza the first questions, the young woman held up an index finger in the universal signal for "hang on a second". Eliza reached into her small red leather purse and withdrew a slim brass cigarette case and a Zippo that looked like it had been through the wars. Eliza offered Peggy a cigarette, which she gladly took, deciding then and there that her goal in the future, once she became wildly famous and brilliantly wealthy was to invest in a cigarette case. It felt dashingly sophisticated and much chicer than to simply carry them in the carton, as Peggy herself did. Peggy was interested in the Zippo. It seemed to stand out so phenomenally in opposition to Eliza's other effects that there must be a story attached to it. A hidden and curious sentimentality must keep Eliza attached to the battered thing when she clearly valued classy, smart items. Once the cigarettes were lit, Eliza indicated with the same index finger to carry on with the questionnaire.

"Your name is Eliza Lynton," Peggy began, to which Eliza nodded her chestnut head, "Marital status?"

Eliza held up her left hand and showed Peggy the beautiful ruby and gold ring on her fourth finger, and beamed, before answering "Engaged! Set to be married next June!" Peggy felt the blood rush from her face and down to her toes. Her heart sank, and her voice cracked when she congratulated Eliza and wished her many happy returns on her wedding day. After that, Peggy wasn't sure how she managed to complete the rest of the questionnaire. The words were a blur, and Eliza's answers and questions swam together in her head. After what felt like an eternity, Peggy excused herself to the ladies' room, leaving Eliza sitting at the table with a concerned look on her face.

Peggy locked the door to the restroom behind her. Engaged. Engaged. Engaged. Eliza was engaged. That meant John was engaged. That meant her silly, childish thoughts had been directed at another woman's fiancé. She slid down the door until she was sitting on the cold, filthy purple and white tile floor. She realized she was still holding the cigarette, and sucked hard at it, inhaling as much smoke into her lungs as she could, before stubbing out the butt onto the tile floor. Mrs. Brennan would have had a conniption if she had seen her daughter seated on the floor of a public restroom, butting out her cigarette anywhere other than in an ashtray. Peggy placed her cold hands to her clammy, cold cheeks, and tried to take a deep breath. She was angry with herself for feeling so upset. Over a man. Her boss, no less. Peggy had always determined that she would not be like other women. She would never allow a man to derail her. She would never be simply a wife. She would never lose herself into children. She would never gaze wistfully out the window at the blue mountains, as her mother had done, time and time again, wishing that she had fulfilled herself. Wishing that her life did not revolve around a tent-like maternity dress, a baby on the floor and an ironing board in the kitchen. She wanted to be at the office, like her father, like all the Important Men. She wanted to be the Important Woman, not Mrs. Important Man. She picked herself up off the floor and ran the cold water into the sink. She took a paper towel and, dipping it in the water, dabbed her face, careful not to cause her mascara to run. She looked hard into her green eyes, ignoring the pallor of her cheeks, causing her freckles to stand out so glaringly.

"You, Margaret Anne Brennan, are not in love with John Grant. You barely know him. You share common interests and beliefs, but the only reason that you need him in your life is to get your byline. He is free to marry whomever he chooses, and you are not to be upset about this. Pull yourself together, go back to your table and do your job," Peggy spoke to her reflection with such ferocity that she felt the blood begin to circulate through her cheeks again.

She nodded to herself in agreement, smoothed her hair, picked up the cigarette butt from where she had left it, and marched with purpose back to the table and to Eliza Lynton, the beautiful betrothed.

20

"Of course, the grooviest bit was when Elizabeth Montgomery actually bought the skirt I suggested. I mean really bought the skirt. It ain't every day that I am helpin' dress the It Girl of the year, ya know!"

Rita was holding forth at the dinner table when Peggy shook the snow off o her coat and hung it on the coat rack. The rack looked like an overburdened hostess, laden with damp heavy outerwear, waiting for a chance to run off to dump her burden on the guest bed. Peggy laid her hat over the vent and stepped out of her salt-crusted boots. She contemplated skipping dinner and heading straight to her cozy nook, but her stomach grumbled, making the decision for her.

"Peggy Sue!! We were starin' ta think you weren't comin'! Busy day at the office? C'mon! I was just tellin' the girls about my day!" Rita's eyes sparkled with excitement, her cheeks pink from the warmth of the room, or the glass of wine.

Peggy smiled at her friend as she found her seat. As usual, Rita's outfit was a sight to behold. Acid green nylon blouse, layer upon layer of necklaces, including a peace symbol, a victory sign, and the symbol for female, her hair, bereft of its usual beehive, was parted down the center and a leather thong wrapped around her forehead, as Peggy had seen the hippies in the news wear.

"What was your exciting news?" although Peggy had heard Rita when she came in, she did not want to deny her friend the excitement of the retelling. Peggy settled herself and gratefully cupped the hot teacup that Mrs. Penske placed in front of her, absorbing the warmth into her cold hands.

"Well, believe it or not, but you'd better believe that I had the most exciting customer in the shop today! My jaw just about hit the floor! But, as I breathe, Elizabeth Montgomery, ya know, the actress from the TV show Bewitched, the pretty one? Samantha? Well, didn't she just come into the store? And not only that, but she actually bought a skirt that I suggested. I mean really bought it! My god but isn't she just as pretty in life as she is on the TV! I mean, she's a bit skinnier than I expected, but ya know they say the camera adds ten pounds. Just as sweet as can be. My goodness!" Rita took another sip of her wine, as Anya carried the roasting pan from the kitchen and placed it on the table. The three chickens lay side by side, glistening and smelling seductively of rosemary, pepper, and crackling fat. Mrs. Penske laid a green Pyrex bowl of smooth mashed potatoes and a gravy boat of pale ivory chicken gravy next to the pan.

Peggy's mouth watered as the dish was passed around, and more dishes of Brussels sprouts, fried turnips and yams were added to the feast. Almost as much as Peggy loved her cozy window, she relished in the fine foods that she enjoyed under Mrs. Penske's roof. She knew of some girls who boarded at other houses where the fare was not nearly as appetizing. Some girls lived on Swanson dinners, and she knew they missed the comfort of a home cooked meal, the feeling of joining around the table for conversation. Her need to observe was fulfilled as she looked around the table at the women who made her home. Shaking off the day became easier as she listened to Rita chat. She looked at Kate, her face broken in a genuine smile as she listened, and nodded, her long hair streaming down her back. Mary's pixie features twinkled, and she waited for her opportunity to get in a word edgewise.

"Ummm, I have something to tell you all," Mary squeaked as Rita stopped talking long enough to take a bite of her chicken. All eyes turned to Mary, who tugged nervously at a curl behind her ear. Her cheeks colored prettily, and she licked her dainty lips and took a deep breath. "I, um, I..." at a loss for words, she lifted her left hand and showed the ladies the large diamond on her ring finger. It was all Peggy could do to stop herself from rolling her eyes. For the second time in one day, Peggy felt sidelined by a ring. She slumped back in her seat and pushed the food around on her plate with her fork moodily. She did not even try to muster a wane smile, as the other girls jumped out of their chairs to hug and congratulate Mary, oohing and aahing over the ring.

Peggy was sitting her usual spot nestled in her afghan, gazing out her window up at the sky. For the first night in weeks, the sky was crystalline. The moon shone so brightly that the street was bathed in a silvery glow which almost eliminated the need for the streetlamps. Around the moon, the aura sparkled prismatically, and Peggy smiled at the memory of sitting around a bonfire when she was about seven years old, looking up at the night sky, as she rested her cheek on Mr. Brennan's scratchy woolen buffalo coat. He explained that on a clear night, the aura of the moon was illuminating ice crystals in the sky. She remembered picturing tiny diamond-like crystals floating high in the sky and wishing that her Daddy could just pull down a few for her. She remembered the acrid smell of the damp wool, mixed with the smell of tobacco, the smoke from the fire, and the musk of her father's aftershave. Roused from her reverie by a faint knocking at her door, she called for whomever it was to come in. There, framed in a halo of light from the hall sconce, Mary stood, meekly biting her bottom lip, with downcast eyes.

"May I come in, Peggy?" she asked, uncharacteristically quiet. Peggy was reluctant to talk to her friend, as she knew that she could not offer her the great excitement that the other girls in the house did.

Feeling she could hardly deny her, she patted the space in front of her on the window seat, just beside her tucked up feet. Mary gently shut the door behind her and crossed the room. Her blue flannel housecoat matched the blue of her eyes exactly and Peggy was struck, once again, but the sheer beauty of her cherubic friend. Mary sat stiffly on the edge of the bench, not snuggling into the space across from Peggy. Whether this was from nerves or lack of familiarity with the room, Peggy could not discern.

"You were quiet tonight," Mary ventured. Peggy

steeled herself for what she expected to come next.

"Yes," Peggy affirmed.

"I think you are upset," Mary glanced sidelong at Peggy, rolling her new engagement ring uncomfortably between her fingers.

"What right have I to be upset?" asked Peggy.

"I did not say whether or not you had the right to be upset, only that I think you are upset. Sometimes, we are upset, rightly or wrongly," Mary spoke quietly, tipping her chin towards Peggy, slightly.

Peggy bit her lip, and took an unnecessary sip of her tea, allowing herself a further moment to gather her thoughts. She knew if she spoke her mind, she risked losing Mary as a friend, and she could not stand for that, but her own personal pride kept her from saying what she thought Mary would want to hear.

"Alright, I admit that I am not over the moon about all of this. You're only 18. You're in college. You have your whole life to get married. Why would you want to do this now? What about your education? What about your life?" she finished dramatically, reaching out her hands to clasp Mary's in her own.

"It's not necessary that I finish my education now. I mean, what's the point? Ed is a dentist, with his own practice. I expect it will take a little while to get settled, but once we are, I hope to have babies straight away. Ed wants that, too. He wants his kids to have a new baby brother or sister to love!"

"His kids? Ed is divorced?" Peggy was taken aback by this news.

"No, he's a widower. He has three darling little ones, Fiona, Felix, and Felicity. They are just grasping for a mother. It's been awfully hard on the children since their mother died, and Ed can't have his sister stay to take care of them forever. She's already stayed over a year, and needs to get back to her own life," Mary said earnestly.

"Mar, ummm, don't think me terribly rude, but just how old is Ed the dentist?" It had never occurred to Peggy to ask this in the months that Mary had been seeing him, assuming that he must be a young man, as Mary was such a sweet young woman.

Mary assumed the pose of indignation, a look Peggy recognized well, as she was a master of indignation herself.

"He's not old! He's only a little older than me, he just happens to have children!" Mary skirted the question, and Peggy raised her right eyebrow questioningly. "He's only thirty-eight!"

"Thirty-eight?" Peggy exclaimed louder than she meant to, "but Mary! That's twenty years older than you! He's old enough to have served!" Peggy pictured a near-doddering old man, with white hair poking out below the surgeon's headlamp, with a white dentist's coat, bedecked with medals from the last war, a cane, and a gaggle of children following him, and Mary tottering along, pushing a pram laden with babies. Peggy's green eyes widen in surprise.

"Oh hush! It's not so bad! And it really is a good position for me – children to keep me busy, a house to keep, and a good solid income," Mary ticked off the pros on one hand, whilst the engagement ring glinted on her left hand.

"You're making this sound like a job! Keep you busy, solid income! Not one word about love! If you are marrying him for something to do, why not complete your education and find yourself a suitable job as a secretary, as you wanted? Or anything! You could become a flight attendant and see the world! There is so much you could do! You really mustn't throw away your life like this!" Peggy felt her face flush as she jumped headlong into exactly what she had hoped to keep herself from saying.

"It is not a job, although I think that being a housewife and mother to three little ones, and however many more may come along to be the noblest of jobs. It is not throwing my life away, as you put it, it is making a choice to have the life that I want. Not everyone wants to push and scrape and work as you do, Peggy. Some of us want what our mothers had – a happy home and a good provider. Ed will be a good provider, and I will be a happy housewife. And to say that I think nothing of love is not true. How many times have I not mentioned falling in love with Ed over these months? I do love him, very much, and I do not care in the least that he is twenty years older than me. He loves me, and I love him. He is a good man, and I am happy that I am to be his wife, and I really, truly hope that as my friend you will try to be happy for me!" Mary had risen to her feet, looking every bit the precocious Tinker Bell with her fists jammed into her hips, and her tiny chin tilted up, looking down at Peggy from over her upturned nose.

"There, there, dear, please sit," Peggy reached for Mary's hand again, and used the words her mother had used to soothe her out a temper so many times in her life. Mary allowed herself to be coaxed into sitting again but kept the fierce expression. "I'm sorry I was so harsh. It just makes me sad to see women return to the home and give up on their own ambitions. Or worse, pretend that they do not have ambitions, and squelch whatever they may have wanted. Women aren't even asked what we want. We aren't asked, so we don't think about it, and we just allow ourselves to be shepherded into a life that we did not design." She felt Mary stiffen and realized that this was not helping her cause.

"Mary, if you are happy, I will be happy for you," Peggy said placatingly. She felt Mary squeeze her hand slightly as if to say that while she did not fully forgive Peggy her beliefs, she appreciated the sentiment and Peggy's efforts to avoid a row. "So, when is this blessed event to take place?"

Mary smirked at Peggy's sardonic tone, and relaxed.

"A month from Saturday. To give Mother and Father a chance to come to the City, and for the girls and I time to select dresses. It's going to be a small thing, really. Just family and close friends. We are going to meet with the Reverend tomorrow morning before Ed goes to work. Of course, I wish that we could have my minister from home, after all, he married Ma and Pa, but some things are simply not manageable, so I'll have to be happy with Mr. Dawes," Mary said, tugging her curl again with a sigh.

"Have you called home and asked them about

bringing your preacher out here?" Peggy asked.
"Preacher? Oh, Peggy, you do say the funniest
things! He isn't a preacher; he is a Vicar!" Mary
burst out in peals of laughter.

"Well, where I come from, any man of the cloth is a
preacher. You're lucky I don't stroll around without
a piece of hay between my teeth," teased Peggy, with
a laugh. In her hometown, there was one Methodist
Church, one Baptist Church, and one Catholic
Church, and around town, be he a Reverend, a
Pastor or a Priest, the church leaders were called
preachers, or 'the preacher man' if he was talking to
Old Man Gower. She remembered the three men
sitting amiably in the town cafeteria, sharing a coffee
and discussing the finer points that kept them from
having the same faith, regardless of the fact that they
all believed in the same God and that they all
believed that Jesus died for their sins. She always
felt that those meals were an example of brotherly
love and that if more people followed the examples
of those three men, the world would be a much
kinder place.

"That sounds like a place straight out of a John
Wayne film!" Mary laughed at the image but did
not know how close to the truth that really was.
Peggy was not from the Wild West, but she was
certainly from a town small enough to be described
as 'one horse'. "You must have felt just like Dorothy
when you got here! The Emerald City stretched as

far as the eye could see! But no, I did not ask the Reverend Michaels to preside, as that would be such an inconvenience to him, and besides, there isn't going to be much fuss. Ed feels that would be unseemly for a second marriage. He would hate for people to have the wrong impression of him."

"But, honey, it's your first marriage. Shouldn't it be special for you, too? It isn't your fault that he's been married before," Peggy asked. She was beginning to feel that she was at the end of her ability to show patience for this match. She had not even met Ed or his gaggle of F children, and he was already wearing on her nerves. If he was going to marry an 18-year-old girl, instead of hiring a nanny for his children, the least he could do was give her a proper wedding.

"Thank you, Peggy. But it will be special. It will be my wedding day. There is nothing more special than marrying the man I love, before the eyes of God and my family," Mary said, patting Peggy's leg, and rising to leave. "Thanks for talking to me, Peg. I would hate for this to drive a wedge between us. You really have been like a sister to me these last months and I would miss you dreadfully if you didn't love me because I got married."

"Oh, Mary! Just because I don't want to get married, and that this wouldn't be my choice, doesn't mean I won't love you!" Peggy jumped up, knocking her blankets and books to the floor, and nearly tipping her teacup over, spilling its contents everywhere. She grabbed Mary to her and hugged her ferociously. Mary hugged her back, and then just as meekly as she had entered the room, she departed.

Peggy thought about what Mary had said about her being like Dorothy, and she realized that that was exactly how she felt. As a little girl, she had fantasized about L. Frank Baum's Wonderful World of Oz, and coming from a tiny place, not unlike the Kansas of the stories, she imagined herself allied with magical friends, who would help her fulfill her dreams at the Emerald City. In her life, she had been the one to help herself through the magical world of Oz. It was her own scrimping and saving and budgeting that had gotten her to this very tiny attic room; it was her own hard work and dedication that had gotten her through her College years and into the typing pool at The Tribune; and she felt that it was her own ability to place herself in opportunity's way that would lead her through the enchanted doors to her own office, and her own byline.

But first, she thought, she must figure out a way to be the Scarecrow to Mary's Dorothy. She settled down to pen a letter.

21

Peggy walked briskly out of the boarding house, with the air of someone who had important things to do. Someone who had a goal in mind. Peggy certainly had a goal, but it was not for where she was going; it was simply to get away from the chaos that was her home, overrun as it was at the moment by children, women and sewing scissors. Mary's soon-to-be sister-in-law had brought the Fearsome F's, as Peggy secretly referred to them, who appeared to her to have had absolutely no parenting since the passing of their mother a year before; Em and Audrey were drill sergeants in the War on Wedding, bossing everyone, including the bride, to within an inch of their lives.

Poor Anya was being treated more like a runner than a housekeeper, as Emily and Audrey directed "Anya, please run and grab..." this, that or the other thing. There were yards and yards of white satin laid out in the sitting room, giving it the look of an underfunded theatre. The phone kept jangling off the hook, as Mary's mother, or sister, or aunt called to offer their suggestions. For a wedding that was meant to be a 'small affair', it certainly seemed to be huge in their home. Peggy's cheeks were pink from the cold and from the exertion of her quick footsteps on the wet walkway. It had not snowed in three days, so the pavement was clear for the first time that week, allowing Peggy to walk without fear of slipping. Rounding the block away from the house, Peggy arrived at the busier main road, and continued along, towards to shoppers rushing in and out of merchants with their Christmassy wares. She considered joining them and procuring the gifts she would send home over the holidays to her family. She slowed her pace and felt the now familiar pang of homesickness at the thought that she would not be joining in the merriment of a Brennan Family Christmas this year. She imagined that Mrs. Brennan would be feeling forlorn this year, as she liked to have all of her children and their families home from December 21st until January 2nd, no matter what was happening in their lives. The family teased her about her traditions, but they all knew and appreciated that they could count on their mother to be simmering golden gravy, roasting butternut squash and a crispy, succulent turkey, to be followed by pumpkin, pecan and apple pie; for there to be glittering lights on the fresh scented tree; for the packages to be neatly wrapped and tucked carefully under the boughs. This was the definition of Christmas to every one of the Brennan children, and they had never spent the holiday apart. But this year, Peggy was in the city, and could not afford the train fare home, Linda was in San Francisco, and none of the family knew how to get in touch with her, and it was unlikely that she would miraculously appear at the solid oak door at the Brennan family home. Peggy could see her and her sisters, cuddled under one of Mrs. Brennan's homemade afghans, giggling and sharing popcorn, while Harry and George wrestled with the dogs on the carpet before the fireplace. She pictured her father, with his sweet tobacco pipe, in his easy chair reading his favourite Dickens novel. She saw Mama coming in and out of the room, commanding the boys to stop harassing the poor dog, and telling the girls that it was the time that someone in this family learned to make the stuffing. Over the years, more people had joined the family, and the idyllic family tableau changed, as George married Nancy, then they had their babies, bringing a new element to Christmas, that Mrs. Brennan adored; then Joan had married John Michael, and her four children became the centerpiece of Christmas, and finally, Linda had married Tom, and the dining table had become so overcrowded that there was frequent elbowing throughout the holiday meals. Peggy did not resent the intrusion of these interlopers, per se, but she missed the family of seven. The Original Brennans, as she secretly thought of them. Perhaps it was her lack of interest in the babies and children, or perhaps she simply missed the simpler days gone by.

As Peggy passed the shops, she glanced into the windows, at the festive displays. She marveled at the décor in some of the larger department stores and could not believe how far she had come in a year. Slowing her pace, she caught her breath and began

to wander. The sky was a brilliant blue, with wisps
of cloud streaked across. The lack of cloud cover
had produced a vivid sunny day, but along with it, a
biting cold. Peggy was certain that it would have to
warm up at least five degrees in order to be warm
enough to snow. As she walked, she noticed a
narrow storefront that she had not seen before. It
must have been there for ages, as the building was
sooty, and the paint was peeling from the sign above
the door. In the window, a row of sun-faded books
was gathering dust, a stark contrast to the gorgeous
displays on either side of it. Peggy could see past
the books, into a dark, dingy space, with shelves
stacked to the high ceilings with books. She tried
the door and found it open, though stubborn. She
tugged and nearly lost her footing as the door
released from its jamb. Peggy was instantly
overcome with the scent of musty, slightly damp
books. She stepped onto a worn maroon carpet that
looked like it had been greeting customers since the
wars. Before her was a great table piled four feet
high with books. To say they were stacked would be
a disserve to stacks everywhere. These books
looked more like they had been tossed haphazardly
onto the table over the course of decades, and
rather than sort through and organize, the
shopkeeper had simply thrown more and more
books onto the heaping mound. She heard a faint
tinkle as the door shut behind her. Taking tentative
steps, Peggy moved past the table, towards the
shelves, thinking that it was a wonder that they did

not topple over. She read the names on the spines that she could see: Machiavelli, slotted next to Austen, who leaned against Friedan. Peggy scrunched her freckled nose at this strange ordering. How could anyone hope to find anything in this jumble? She was conscious that if she were to be in charge of setting up a bookstore, this would likely be her system as well. The mess and clutter felt homey to her. She could imagine her mother and Joanie in this place. She giggled audibly at the imagined looks of horror and disgust that the two women who were strong proponents of tidiness would surely have had. She ran her gloved finger along the dusty spines and smiled to herself. Orwell, Lewis, Steinbeck, Waugh, Isherwood, Highsmith. They were evidently not sorted by alphabetical order, nor by genre. They were just there, in the store, for readers to find. It was like a treasure hunt. She turned when she heard the murmur of voices behind her. She saw a hunched, elderly woman beside a tall, young man. The woman was leaning on a classroom pointer, as though it were a cane. The young man leaned in to speak to her and she coughed, frowned and then nodded. Lifting the pointer, she spun around and directed it to a shelf above the young man's head and tapped on the shelf.

"It's there. Go ahead and slide the ladder over here. That one, there. There's a good lad. You go on up. This old body does not climb that ladder anymore. I am sure you noticed the table when you came in. Well, anything that I can't reach anymore goes on there," she nodded her blue-gray head as she spoke, leaning on the pointer once more. The young man climbed the ladder agilely and reached for a book.

"Son of a gun, ma'am! How did you know? I have never seen the likes of it!" He held the book aloft as he jumped back to the floor, striking Peggy the resemblance of a cat.

"Well, young man, you work in a store as long as I have worked here, and you would certainly remember where things are. No use asking about what if it is sold. If it were sold, I would have told you so. I don't go around on any wild goose chases anymore and I certainly would not send my customers on them either,' she rapped the pointer on the carpet twice, and then turned towards Peggy, and began ambling down the aisle. "Hello, young lady. Can I help you find anything?"

Peggy smiled at her, then at the young man, in turn. "I'm just looking but thank you. I apologise for eavesdropping, but I couldn't help overhearing. Why do you not hire some help? Certainly, you would like to have order in your store?"

The old woman tipped her head back and let out a great guffaw. "Order? In this store? Ha! There has never been order in this store. From the day my dearly departed husband bought the first set of books to grace these shelves until today, there has never been a smidgen of order. You see, my husband had an idea that being a shopkeeper was a dignified profession, and so, he bought this building, and we set up house upstairs. He built shelves and decided that it would be very prestigious if he could buy and sell old books from estate sales. The dear heart loved to buy books, but he could not organize a thing to save his life. Raising kids in a bookstore does not add to organization as Mikey would pull a book down, and move it to another shelf, or Karen would build castles out of books on the floor. So, what was the point? There was no point then, and there is no point now," The old woman's cloudy gray eyes looked at Peggy from her wizened face, and her smile revealed ancient wooden teeth, interspersed with the occasional yellowing natural tooth. Despite the crone-ish appearance, Peggy found herself drawn to the woman.

She smiled back and glanced up at the young man's face. He smiled at her, and tipped his hat, like John Wayne.

"How long has the store been here? I have never noticed it before, and I have been living around the block for months," Peggy asked, following the small woman, and the man to the ancient desk at the back of the darkly lit, confined shop.

At her feet were piles of books propped against

each other, so Peggy felt the need to watch her step for fear of tripping. Peggy thought she could see little clouds of dust raised from the carpet every time her black leather boot trod down. Was it possible that this little creature, the pointer in hand, was the sole caretaker of this mausoleum of literature?

"Store's been here nigh on 50 years. Opened the doors in 1915, kept going through the Depression, by the will of God, through the Second World War, when my Mikey was called up to serve. Karen helped me in those days," the old woman drew out a metal cash box from under a pile of newspapers, and some dogeared paperback novels and set about fishing around in the pocket of her rough green army sweater. She soon retrieved a tiny, tarnished silver key and unlocked the box. Peggy's green eyes widened with astonishment, for she had not seen a store that operated solely out a small cashbox since she was a little girl, sitting on a stool in her grandmother's fruit stand by the side of the road.

"After Abel – that's my husband- died, bless him, and Karen had too many babies to bring round the store every day, it was just me. My Mikey was shot down, you see, so he never made it back, God rest his soul."

Peggy was surprised to be given this information so freely, considering that she still did not know the proprietress' name. This was usually the sort of thing that Peggy concocted for herself when meeting a woman like this or finding herself in a place like this. She watched the woman complete her sale with the young man, who tipped his hat again to Peggy and the woman, and then, wrapping his scarf against the cold, stepped out into the sunlit street. Peggy was watching the woman count the money into the box, and then locking it again, she proceeded the return the newspapers and paperbacks to their previous homes on top of the cash box. She saw Peggy watching her, and tapping the side of her bulbous nose, she whispered insurance and winked a smoky eye. Peggy shook her head in amazement. She had not met such a woman in ages.

"I'm Peggy Brennan," she said, extending her long gloved hand to the old woman behind the counter. The woman shifted the pointer to her other hand, and clasping Peggy's replied, "Mrs. Abel Tate. Pleased to make your acquaintance, Miss Brennan."

Peggy felt the familiar cringe to hear a woman refer to herself by her husband's first name, hating the loss of identity that woman had endured through the years.

22

Peggy was sitting at the large table, head bent over her notes, waiting for John and the executives to enter the boardroom. She was anxious to lay the first column to bed, and this was their chance to pitch the first story, written by Caro, typed by Peggy, and edited by Mrs. Kelly. They had chosen a topic that felt bland to Peggy, but eventually, she conceded that warming the executives up to the idea of the column was prudent. She just hoped that they would eventually be free to begin the column that John had originally brought her onboard to. Something daring and bold, something that let other women like herself know that they were not alone. She rubbed her hands together, the chill in the large room causing goosebumps on her arms. She heard chatter beyond the glass paneled door and stood to greet the arrivals. First, in the room, The Decision-Making Men followed quickly by The Secretaries, whose uniform seemed to consist of narrow pencil skirts, blouses tied at the neck, and sleek French twists. The Men nodded to Peggy as they scattered around the table, with The Tribune's owner sitting at the head of the table, unironically under a large painted portrait of himself. The Secretaries filed in behind them and sat on the hard wooden chairs lining the walls, with their notepads perched on their laps. Peggy was about to retake her seat when she felt the slightest touch on her elbow. She turned to see an imperious woman with dark-rimmed glasses and a scowl that seemed to be etched into her skin standing very close to her.

"Excuse me, Miss. I think that you would be more comfortable over there," The Scowl said to Peggy, pointing a red lacquered nail towards a hard wooden chair near the door. Peggy arched her eyebrow and pursed her lips. The likelihood of being more comfortable on a small wooden chair, versus the plush armchair at the table, seemed slight, but Peggy doubted this had much to do with her own comfort and more to do with the status quo.

"Thank you for your concern, but I am fine right here," Peggy said crisply and sat with her back erect in her original place. She heard a humph of disapproval from The Scowl but refused to be concerned.

"I'm sorry I am late. Traffic was a nightmare," John said, as he strode into the room and took his seat next to Peggy.

She was relieved to have someone on her side. Peggy observed the room, as John removed his hat and began to disassemble the contents of his briefcase. The men at the table had settled into deferential poses, heads tilted towards Mr. Brennan, Sr., as though desperate to absorb any nuggets of information that he might have for them, desperate to bump their table positions ever so slightly closer, until they took the position of Right Hand Man. The present Right-Hand Man was an older gentleman, in a brushed charcoal suit. Greying temples and a grey and black mustache, Right Hand Man, tapped quickly on the table with a sterling silver arrow pen, glancing around the room, willing the occupants to come to order, before he received the expected eyebrow raise from Mr. Grant, Sr., alerting him to call them to attention. At the head of the table, under his over-large self-portrait, Mr. John Grant, Sr, known to his few friends and many wives as Jack, sat looking at Peggy with a curious face. She could feel his eyes on her and refused to lower hers in deference when they met. As was her wont, in uncomfortable situations, Peggy pursed her lips, and tipped up her chin, eyeing Jack Grant steadily. Compared to the portrait, Mr. Grant, Sr had become jowly, and the slick black helmet of hair looked more like a henna rinse than the blue-black of the portrait hair. Peggy wondered if the painting had been commissioned more than thirty years ago, or if the painter had been paid extra to show the subject in a more favourable light. The aquiline nose in the painting had become rather red and bulbous in practicality, with his fingers stained yellow from decades of cigar smoke. Peggy began to search for a sign that this codgerly fellow was related to the handsome John Grant that sat next to her. The man in the portrait and the man at the table both wore the same haughty expression that she had never seen cloud

John's face; the portrait had the same bright blue
eyes and dark hair, and Peggy thought that the chin
and lips were very much like John's; however the
man at the end of the table seemed much too old
and much too loathsome to be John's father. The
man to Jack's left wore a sharp three-piece suit, had
blonde hair that held waves, dark, narrow eyes, and
a hooked nose. Peggy felt that the three Decision
Making Men looked rather like a trio of
nightmarish figures that would have haunted her
dreams as a little girl. She wished her mother was
there so that she might point to them and say "HA!
I did not have an overactive imagination! Such men
do stroll the Earth!" Across from her, sat a long row
of men whom she could only describe as pencil-
pushers; she did not know why they were there,
other than as an act of theatre – a prop designed to
intimidate those who sat opposite.

"Well, John, what have you brought us, besides this
pretty little thing?" said Right Hand Man, with a
lascivious wink to Peggy. She felt repulsed and had
to work to keep the physical representation of
disgust from playing across her features. She
glanced quickly to the women lining the room, but
if she had been hoping for a feminine ally, she had
come to the wrong place. These women were
clearly indoctrinated into their roles and had no
qualms about men making inappropriate
comments. In fact, if one were to be surveyed, she
might argue that it was not inappropriate at all, but
rather a par for the course.

"I am sure you can see, Virgil, that I did not bring you a pretty young thing, but rather have been accompanied by Miss Brennan, a highly competent and talented member of my team. We shall be joined momentarily by Miss Caro Nance, who has also agreed to allow her byline to appear in our column," John spoke coolly and levelly to Right Hand Man, who evidently went by the name of Virgil. She noticed the Left-Hand Man roll his narrow eyes.

"Caro, eh? You approved of the use of the cupcake writer to go on over, did ya, Jack?" said Left Hand Man, to Mr. Grant, Sr. He scribbled something onto the yellow legal pad in front of him as he spoke. Before Jack could reply, John spoke again, in the same cool tone.

"Caro is not a cupcake writer, as you well know, Joshua. She is young, but you will remember that she made a name for herself recently when she broke the bus strike in June. She will bring just the right balance of femininity and drive that we hope will engage our readers going forward." Peggy was impressed by John's interest in defending the women he had selected for his department. She knew he had a passion for it but given his clear disdain for working in his father's company, she had thought it would be unlikely that he would be willing to fight the powers that be in any substantial way.

"Yes, yes, John. Get on with it. Where is your

wunderkind?" said his father with a dismissive wave of his mottled hand.

"She is in the middle of interviewing our first subject for the column, and unfortunately, as Joshua and Virgil were adamant that this was the only time that you could all three meets with us, Miss Nance shall be fashionably late," John spoke the two men's names pointedly, as though they had been unreasonable up to now. Suddenly Peggy's brow furrowed as she thought that perhaps John had been sincere in telling her that they needed to make headway slowly with the board. She had assumed that that was simply good old sexism. She did not realize that John had been combatting the sexism himself, just to bring her to the table. She glanced at him, before clearing her throat to speak.

"I am confused, gentlemen. I thought that this was a column that The Tribune was in need of, to bring women to the paper. I am feeling that this is not how you see it?" Peggy tapped the pen on her lip after she spoke and raised her eyebrow questioningly.

"Well, we certainly are in favour of added readership, whether it is of the male or female variety. I do not quite understand why young Mr. Grant here feels that the ladies need more than simply the pages that currently exist. Ask Ada and the recipe feature has always been very popular with my wife. Why would she want to read an interview with Betty Friedan or a bunch of Women's

Movement girls? They have so little in common with her that they might as well be Amazon tribesman," Virgil spoke slowly to Peggy, and then gathered steam, before finishing with what Peggy felt was a laughable apropos mention about tribesmen when referring to women.

Before John could reply, Peggy interjected.

"Gentlemen, who amongst you has a daughter?" Peggy looked at each of their faces in turn, ignoring the tsking from the secretaries lining the wall behind her.

"Young lady, I am not sure that that has to do with it," said Joshua, with a disapproving look. "Please, sir, just bear with me," said Peggy, with her most winning smile. She knew these men would reply more happily to a smiling pretty young thing than to an angry woman. She despised having to play this game in order to get ahead, as she was certain no man would be put in this position, but she knew that she had to gain her footing first before she could make an impact.

Mr. Grant, Sr., patronized her with a fatherly smile, before replying that yes, most of the men at the table had at least one daughter and that Mr. Simpson had four. Peggy looked across the table to the man who chuckled and nodded knowingly.

"Mr. Simpson," Peggy said, directing her attention to the man that was most likely outnumbered by females in his home. "Do your daughters want to grow up to be housewives? Do you have ambitions for them?"

"Well, my third girl, Sherri, she says she wants to be the President one day," Mr. Simpson paused as the other men guffawed loudly and shook their heads at the notion of a tiny woman taking on the power of the nation, and then continued, "I would have thought it was ridiculous, but then I think about Congressman Martha Griffiths and wonder if it really might be possible."

"There is a big difference between a Congressman and the President, Stan," remarked Virgil, condescendingly.

John jumped in and said, "That's true, Virgil, but who knows? Maybe when little Sherri grows up, there will be women running the country. And perhaps adding a little more depth and a little more grit to what women read and have access to would create a sense that there are more options for women, other than whether to use Kraft cheese in their casseroles."

"Well, alright, we will wait for Miss Nance to arrive, and she can present the "grit" you want to add, and then we will make a decision," said Mr. Grant, Sr., nodding to his son. John half smiled in return and began pulling pages from his black leather briefcase. Peggy knew they were mock-ups based on the ideas of the women they had interviewed. She and John had sat late into the night on the floor of his office, with jars of liquid rubber, brushes, and scissors, creating them for the past week. She glowed at the memory of the cold floor, the rasping of scissors, and the friendly chatter between her and John. She was finding it easier to let her guard down, the more she worked with him. She no longer felt the need to rebuff everything he said and began to share control of the conversation.

"Hi, All!" said Caro Nance as she sauntered into the room. Caro was unflappable, regardless of arriving later than anyone else. She wore a sleek houndstooth dress, silk stockings, and a tightly tailored blazer of matching houndstooth, with scarlet piping around the cuffs and collar. At her throat, she wore a short necklace of large plastic beads, the exact shade of the piping. She pulled out a chair, and after a glance around the room sat with the smile of the pageant queen she had been in Missouri. "Thanks for waiting for me, I had to finish a pesky little interview. Oh, are these the mock-ups? Lovely! Let's get started!"

23

"I just can't believe it", cried Emily into Rita's shoulder, as Peggy sat across from them holding the tissue box, "we were going to be getting ENGAGED!!! How could he decide that I wasn't a 'good fit'?" Emily wailed, while Peggy handed her another tissue. Emily's red, blotchy, tear-streaked face was swollen and incredulous.

"There, there, Em darling!" said Rita, nuzzling Emily's hair and rubbing her back, "Teddy is a rat. No need to worry yourself over that ninny!"

"Emily, what did he say... exactly? You have been together for so long that I cannot imagine why you would suddenly be a bad fit. It seems so strange!" Peggy assumed what she imagined was a concerned expression, trying to mask her relief that there would be at least one fewer trip down the aisle in her gang than she had anticipated.

Emily set her jaw, frowned and wailed "it was that awful woman! That... that... that ice queen! Mrs. Laurel! Teddy said that Mr. Laurel was keen to see him in their company, but that his tiresome witch of a wife said I was too common for them, and that Teddy would be wise to leave his childhood behind him!!! Common! What is this, feudal England? Does Teddy think he is Prince Charles? I thought he loved me, and he promised me a certain type of life. Why would he do this?"

Rita could no longer keep her mouth closed and grabbed Emily roughly by the shoulders and shouted "Common?" in her thickest accent. "Common? Are ya serious, darling? You are not common! What the hell kinda nonsense is he spewing! If he can throw you over for some... some... job, then he is no man at all." Peggy nodded in agreement, as Rita, spitting mad stuttered over the thought that beautiful, bright, and clever Emily might be in anyway maligned.

"Em, dear," said Peggy, cocking her pretty head to one side, and passing Emily a tissue, "I am so sorry that you are blue. He was awful to do this to you but just think – now you don't have to live your life around his schedule and plans! You can do anything that you want now. Your life is ahead of you and up to you!" Peggy smiled at Em, expecting a smile of acknowledgement that she no longer had to adapt herself to Mr. Uncommon in return, and instead found herself the unwitting recipient of Emily's hurt feelings and dashed hopes.

"Peggy, dear," Emily nearly spat the endearment, as her plump, tear splotched cheeks redden furthermore, "I am not a... a... a... man-hater like you!!! I wanted to marry Teddy. That was my life. That was my goal! I had a dream, a beautiful, pink castle in the sky, with our two children, our little dog, a big yard, and pink Royal Memory Lane China!" She tightened her fists until her knuckles were white, and Peggy could imagine the long, perfectly lacquered red nails digging into the soft flesh of her hands. Her chest swelled in anger as she began to heave short, shallow breaths through her slightly too large nose. Peggy saw through the timorous lip that she had spoken too soon. She really did have to work on her penchant for bursting forth with whatever thought occurred to her, or rather her judgment of how other women ought to run their own lives. She remembered Mrs. Brennan taking her hand, when her sisters would, in her mind, fly of the handle at the merest suggestion by Peggy that they were leading their lives in a less than fulfilling manner.

She remembered her mother's cool touch as she clucked at Peggy and told her "Margaret, it is not for you to decide what is right for others. You have your own thoughts on what you want from life, though heaven knows where you have come up with some of them. Certainly not from me, but that is a discussion for another time. You must learn when to say the things that are on your mind and when to hold that tongue of yours. One of these days, you will say the wrong thing at the wrong time and do irreparable damage."

Peggy thought at that, and every similar instance, that her mother was being ridiculous. But now as she was faced with an angry and broken-hearted Emily, she wondered if perhaps, as she often did, her mother was right. She did bristle at the suggestion that she was a man-hater, after all, she wanted nothing more than to achieve an equal footing with men, she did not hate them. She opened her pink mouth to say as much to Emily, in her own defense, when she saw Rita, over Emily's shoulder, raise her right eyebrow and shake her head ever so slightly; just enough for her white plastic hoop earrings to slap against her neck, and for Peggy to understand that now was not the time to defend herself from baseless attacks on her character. Instead, she straightened her sweater, and said "I'm sorry, Em. I really am. I just know that Teddy will get to Chicago and realize what an awful mistake he has made and come crawling back to you. You have been together for so long."

Peggy sincerely hoped that if Teddy did come crawling back, that Emily would set him out on his ear, and not even consider allowing him back, given that he had proven himself to be a good-for-nothing, who was more interested in making an impression on his boss and his wife than to support the woman he had professed to love for so long.

Emily calmed slightly after Peggy's apology, throwing herself backwards on to her Tiffany blue duvet cover, her dark hair unkempt, as it escaped from the usual confines of its rose hair ribbon. Peggy lay down on one side of her, and Rita laid on the other, propping her head in her hand. "Ya know, Emmy-bean, if that worm ever does come a-crawlin' back, we can have some common enough words ready for him." And with an exaggerated wink of her heavily made-up eye, Rita had both Peggy and Emily laughing, the former gratefully, and the latter ruefully. Peggy looked at the water mark on the ceiling around the frosted glass light fixture above her and her thoughts drifted from Emily to John. John and Eliza. John and Eliza. John was engaged to Eliza. She pursed her lips as she watched a tiny spider cross through the water mark and across the ceiling. She needed to remember that she was going to be a journalist. She was working on a new, exciting section of the paper. She was a valued member of her set, and she could not think about John, her boss, for goodness' sake, in anything other than a professional capacity. She let out a small sound of frustration, and covered her eyes with her hands, elbows pointing towards the ceiling. She pretended not to notice when she heard the rustle of the duvet next to her, indicating that Emily had turned towards her at the sound she had uttered.

"Who wants some wine? I think that is just what we need to get out of this funk," exclaimed Rita in her cheeriest voice. Peggy quite literally leapt at the suggestion and was out the door and down the stairs before Rita could say another word.

Peggy slowed as she reached the bottom of the stairs. She instinctively pushed a stray ruddy strand of hair off her forehead and let a puff of a sigh escape her lips. She wondered if what Em had said was true. Was she a man-hater? She thought back to Mama and that wistful stare at the mountains. What she saw in those lovely brown eyes had been, she was sure of it, a wish that she had never shared. A wish that she had given up in order to become wife and mother. Peggy could read people; she knew she could. She was the brightest of the bunch at reading people. She wandered slowly into the kitchen and pulled some of the cut glass goblets out the highest cupboard, where Mrs. Penske kept them. She moved automatically; still lost in the memory of the Mama she had grown up with. Her Mama with her smooth, soothing hands. Her Mama who was always impeccably dressed and could fix a meatloaf in 35 minutes flat. Her Mama who gave up everything to raise the Brennan kids and press Daddy's suits and ties. Peggy took the glasses into the living room and haphazardly dropped the heavy cups onto the scuffed, doilied coffee table. She settled herself on her favourite chair and picked at a bit of lint that had attached itself to her nylons. She wasn't sure why she was so bothered by the title of man-hater. She had spent the last several years trying to move into her father's world. She was going to be the best journalist at the Tribune, and she knew that she was going to be exactly who she wanted to be. But was it possible to have both? Could she have a career and a husband? She could hear Mama's voice in her head "Margaret Anne, why on earth do you need both? Come home. Marry a nice boy. He will take care of you, and you will be happy."

But what if the Mama she heard in her head wasn't really what Mrs. Brennan would have said? What if there really was some wistfulness in her doe eyes when she was left alone in her thoughts, without children crying and begging and pulling at her. Peggy bit her bottom lip and tugged at the hole she had indolently pulled into her tights, regretting her thoughtlessness with her things, as she knew that a new pair of pantyhose would not fit into her pinched budget. Peggy decided that maybe it was time to reach out to her Mama. A slight smile crossed her freckled face as the words "Mother knows best" flitted through her mind, just as the rest of the girls entered the room with a tear-stained Emily and the decanter of wine that had been on the ancient wooden counter in the kitchen.

24

Dearest, darlingest, most delicious of Mamas,

How are you? Things are out of this world around here are unbelievable. I am on my way to being the intrepid ace reporter that you never thought that I should be. Or maybe you did? Mama, I need to ask you a question. I don't know if you will answer me or not, but I need to ask – are you happy? Have you always been happy? Is this what you have always wanted?

I have always had this idea of how you actually felt about your life. You have never said that you wanted more for yourself, more than what women are supposed to want. More than us kids, and Daddy. More than being a good wife. But did you? I know that you had a life before us, but what is your life after us? I wonder sometimes if you understand me more than I thought you did. I used to catch you now and again staring into the distance and I imagined that you had some dream of seeing what was beyond the mountains. An adventure all your own. Did you, Mama? Do you understand how it feels to be unsatisfied?

You have always told me that I was ridiculous when I asked what you were thinking about, but now, I wonder if you would please, please tell me something that I can hold on to in the dark when I am alone and I miss you. I would like to know that you are proud of me, and that you can understand why I have to do this. I would like you to comfort me with the knowledge that even though your idea of what is best for me, or at least what you have always said was best for me was not the only thing that you see for me. I want to be important, and it cannot be important without being on the masthead of the paper.

I have spent so many years imagining that you only saw one life for me, one like my sisters; one like yours, while feeling deep in my heart of hearts that you have wanted more. Please don't slough this off. Please take me request to heart, I need your comfort in a way that you have never felt compelled to do before.

Give Daddy a kiss for me, and I really hope to hear back from you soon, Mama. I may not have a new hat, but I am always your,

Peggy

The sun was shining, and Peggy was idly watching Mr. Not-Quite-Successful brownnose his soon-to-be father-in-law, as she lit a cigarette, waiting for Mrs. Tate to join her the diner. She watched the unsubtle dance of the shiny young man, with the creased suit, and forelock that would not stay slicked back try to impress the man he hoped would agree to hand his daughter over for the price of a cheap gold and diamond band. Peggy decided Mr. Not-Quite-Successful was definitely a diamond person. He would have picked it from the shiny glass case at JC Penney's, knowing that it was the diamond that would impress his soon-to-be father-in-law more than the prettier rings, with less showy gems. Peggy blew a puff of bluish smoke into the air around her head, while the soon-to-be father-in-law's bright blue eyes sparkled with barely contained mirth, cutting into his Salisbury steak.

Peggy was interrupted from her imaginings by the personage of Mrs. Abel Tate, as she dropped on to the booth bench across from Peggy. Peggy had visited the store several times in the past few days, intrigued by the small old woman who had so freely shared her story months ago. The crocuses had begun poking their purple faces through the melting snow, and Mrs. Tate was out of breath from the still cool, new spring air. Peggy had developed an affection for the funny old face, and the homely air that came from her rough soap, and bluing agent, over the must of the old store lingering on her natty orange sweater.

"Good day, Miss. Brennan. It's good to see your face. I am looking forward to hearing all about those interviews you were telling me about. But first, as Abel – God rest his soul – always said, let's see who we need to bribe to get some hot coffee and a bun in this place".

Peggy watched the halo of blue grey fluff around the woman's head catch the sunlight and she could almost swear that she saw rainbows in the strands. She tapped her cigarette into the cheap metal ashtray in the center of the table and smiled.

Once the two women, one wizened, and one plummy and pink, had ordered their coffees and their lunches, they settled into a comfortable chatter, like that of a grandmother with a favoured grandchild. It would be impossible for bystanders to know that the two women had only been in acquaintance since the now-dissolving winter. Peggy regaled Mrs. Tate with stories of interviews, story ideas, gossip from the boarding house, and finally landed on the topic of her mother. Peggy told her about the letter that she had posted, but about which she had yet to hear a reply.

"Peggy, my dear, I think you need to be patient with your mother. It was never in our natures to want things. Let alone to tell our girls about the things that we wanted or did. It was our job to make sure that they were safe and protected." Peggy saw genuine concern in the eyes of the small old woman. She was surprised, because she wasn't seeking concern. She had believed that the dynamic old lady would have seen her side of the story and agreed whole heartedly.

"How can you of all people say that Mrs. Tate? You are a woman who runs her own store in the heart of the city all alone. You surely can't tell me that you don't tell your daughter about the world being more than just babies!" Peggy crinkled her nose, and sipped her coffee, as Mrs. Tate shook her head.

"I didn't start this company on my own. I was left the insurance money by my caring husband – God rest his soul. Karen has all of her babes, and is married in the new neighbourhood outside town, with a big black sedan, and a husband with a big job. I want her to be happy, I want her to be cared for, but I have never given her or her brother any idea that they are anything less than the apples of my eye. Nicky – God rest his soul – would have been married with kids by now, but if he had lived, if he had come home from his flying days, he would be the one running the store and I would be helping his wife care for his babies. Be patient with your mother. She raised you to be strong and brave and independent, so I am sure that in your heart you know that she wanted you to have the life you always dreamed of... nope, there is no point in arguing. You may think that this is on your father, that it was his suit and fedora that got you to the city, but girls are raised by their mothers, and no matter how many hats she wished you had bought, and no matter how many times she begs you to return to Hamilton, she is the reason that you have the fortitude to be having coffee and cigarettes with a silly old biddy that you met in a Christmas-festooned store." Mrs. Tate winked one of her smoky eyes and cut into her bun as though it were a steak. Peggy pursed her lips and leaned back in her seat, tapping one her slender fingers on her lips as she considered what was said. She saw her mother dressing her and caring for her and leading her through her life. She pictured her sewing her dresses and feeding her family. She remembered her small private smile when Peggy bested one of her brothers or her father in an argument. She remembered the way her father would read the paper at the table, and for once, instead of imagining the scene of her wishing she was the reporter bringing the news that Mr. Brennan found more interesting than his family at the white speckled Formica table in their cramped kitchen breakfast nook, she saw her mother. She saw Mrs. Brennan in her curlers, bustling about the kitchen, asking each of her children questions and listening to their answers. Each child treated as though their lives were of the utmost important to at least one parent. Peggy felt the spark of realization that it was her mother who emboldened her and encouraged her in her questioning of the expectations of women. Her mother may not have expected Peggy's goals and dreams to take her so far from home, but her mother had listened as she explained in what may have been excruciating detail for a woman who was methodically peeling two dozen potatoes to feed her family, the angle of her next writing assignment or the grim details of the grisly murder that had been in the morning's paper. Peggy flicked her bright green eyes back onto the face sitting across from her, the bulbous nose hidden in her coffee cup. Peggy leaned forward, resting her elbows on the table between them, she cupped her chin and her eyes widened with surprise.

"Oh, my goodness! Mrs. Tate! Mrs. Tate, I am going to give my mother a call when I get home. How did you know? You've never met my mother, and yet you have made me see her in a whole new light. What if my letter hurt her? I've never made my mother cry before!!" Peggy was startled by the old woman's burst of laughter. "What? What is so funny?"

"Peggy, dear naïve Peggy, you have been making your mother cry since before you were born. There is no child alive who has not brought tears to their mothers. Every day of motherhood is a thousand tiny pains that sometimes are endured, and sometimes are the straw that broke the darn camel's back that draws us to our beds, with a handkerchief."

Mrs. Tate spoke kindly, her round belly and stooped shoulders still rolling with silent laughter. Peggy tucked a tendril of auburn hair behind her left ear and looked closely at Mrs. Tate, as though this funny old woman were a soothsayer opening Peggy's eyes to a blind spot, she had never known she had. It's true that her days were spent in the care of her mother.

Maybe her mother knew what sort of girl Peggy was all along. Maybe her aspirations weren't in spite of Mrs. Brennan but because of her. Could that really be?

26

John took a long drag on his cigarette, then set it back into his thin gold ashtray. Peggy watched him as he read over her newest set of interview notes. She watched for the slightest nod of agreement and felt the petulant shadow of a frown grace her forehead. She found herself watching his bright blue eyes and willing herself to resist pushing the loose forelock back onto his otherwise perfectly groomed head. "Good. These are good, Peg," said John finally. Peg. He had never shortened her name before. She quite liked it. She caught herself wondering if it was a term of endearment, or if it made her 'one of the guys.' In her heart of hearts, she wished for the former, even while telling herself that she preferred the latter.

"Thank you," she replied primly, standing and smoothing the rusty orange cotton of her knee length skirt. She put out her hand for her notes to be returned to her but was surprised when John held her gaze for a moment longer than was entirely necessary.

"You know, my parents are having a dinner party on Saturday night. Lots of people from the newspaper world. Lots of important people for someone who is just starting out to meet. Would you like to join me?" he tilted his head slightly to the right, watching her, and brushing the forelock back into place. Would she care to join him? OF COURSE, she wanted to come! She could meet so many amazing people and really get her name into the world. Her green eyes sparkled with excitement, and she broke into a wide, girlish grin, as though she had been offered free rein in a sweet shop.

"Yes!" she said breathlessly, "Yes, I would love to join you! What is the dress code? What time should I arrive?"

He pulled a pale blue invitation out of his top desk drawer and handed it to her. "All of the information is on there. I'll ring Eliza at Bloomingdale's and ask her to pull you some options."

Peggy flushed. She could not afford a dress from Bloomingdale's, even for a dinner with the Queen. And she certainly did not want John's dear Eliza selecting a dress for her. She would not give anyone the satisfaction of any of these thoughts, though, and as lightly as she could, she waved him off.

"That won't be necessary, Mr. Grant," she said as she turned on her heel, clutching the invitation to her chest, not seeing the look of amusement that John took at her excitement and her haughty exit.

She really did have a conundrum, though. Looking at the delicate silver lettering on the pretty invitation, it was clear that nothing that she owned was up to snuff for this level of dinner party. The dress code was labelled cocktail, and even her finest frock was

not nearly what one would consider cocktail.
Leaving the Tribune typing pool, she headed to the
bank of telephone boxes in the grey marble lobby
and took out her change purse. There was only one
person who could help with this.

"Hello?" answered a warm voice after three rings.

"Hello, Mother," Peggy smiled to hear her voice.

"Margaret! Oh, hello darling! Whatever is wrong?"
Her mother's voice swiftly went front grilled to
concerned as she realized that it was midday and
Peggy ought to be working.
"I need your help. I need a dress for Saturday night,
and I haven't a thing to wear that is appropriate."
Peggy wasn't sure how her mother, hours away by
train, could possibly help her with only four days
until the dinner, but in that moment all that she
knew was that she needed her mother.

"What about your black shift dress? You always
look lovely in it, and as they say, one can never go
wrong in a little black dress."

"No, it's a cocktail party, with some very important
newspaper men, including the owner of the
Tribune." She did not add that John will be there,
as she does not want her dear romantic mother to
get any silly ideas about Peggy falling in love.

"Oh dear. That is a challenge. Let me think on it and
we can chat tonight when you get home from work."

"Thank you, Mother. You are an absolute treasure,"

Peggy blew kisses into the receiver and gently placed the phone back on its hook.

27

At 5pm, as Peggy stepped out the front doors of the Tribune building, she found herself face to face with her mother. Standing neatly under an umbrella, Mrs. Brennan held an emerald overnight case in one hand and appeared to be scanning the faces of each young woman as she bustled out of the building and into the rain.

"Mother?" Peggy gasped and held her hat as she ran through the rain to reach her. "What in heaven's name are you doing here? How did you get here? Where is Father? Where are the kids?"

"I told you I would think on it, and we would chat after you were done work for the day. So, I thought on it, and Daddy and I decided that if our dear independent girl calls in the middle of the day and asks for help, then she must truly need it, and I boarded a train straightaway. Now let's catch a cab back to your boarding house, so we can set this bag down and figure out what we are going to do."

Peggy was overcome with love and joy to see her mother so unexpectedly and in a flash was embracing her mother, the scent of wet wool and her Lilly Dache perfume filling her nose.

Mrs. Penske graciously made up her own spare bedroom for Mrs. Brennan, claiming that it would be nice to have another mother around the house for a few days. Mrs. Brennan efficiently unpacked and then joined Peggy in the parlour, settling herself neatly on one of the wingback chairs near the window.

"So, Margaret dear, tell me about this dinner," Mrs. Brennan leaned forward in her chair and clasped Peggy's slender hands.

"It is being held by the owners of the Tribune and will be the talk of the season," Peggy couldn't help speaking in italics, "the invitation says that it is cocktail attire, and it is being held in the mansion of the Grants. I simply must be there, and I have absolutely nothing to wear. John... I mean Mr. Grant said that I should choose something from Bloomingdale's and that he would have his girlfriend help me choose the gown, but I assure that I am not wearing anything that she selects for me. She may have good taste and all of that, but the dresses in that dress salon start at $60. There is simply no way on earth that I could afford something like that."

Mrs. Brennan cocked her left brow at the mention of 'John' and his 'girlfriend'. She knew better than to say anything, but it sounded like her fiercely independent daughter might just have developed a crush and might be ever so slightly jealous.

"Alright. You are right in that regard. $60 is an awfully large sum for a dress you will only wear once or twice. Are there any sewing and notions stores nearby? Mrs. Penske is bound to have a sewing machine that we can borrow."

"Oh Mother, you know that I am hopeless at sewing, and I have to work everyday between now and the party. I could never bring something together at this rate."

"Dearest, there is a reason that a girl calls her mother in a situation like this. It's true that your strength is with the pen and not the needle, but I could whip something up that would fit in at the most glamorous of tables between now and then. So, tell me, where is there a sewing and notions store? Let's select a pattern, and some elegant soie de chine and get started."

Peggy pulled her mother's hands towards her and kissed them, leaving the slightest trace of apricot lipstick across her knuckles.

28

When Peggy returned from work, she found her mother and Mrs. Penske together, heads bent over the beautiful burnt orange soie de chine fabric that Peggy and her mother had selected the day before. They were carefully pinning and cutting and trimming and laughing together at the dining room table, as though they were old school chums who had reunited for a fun project. Peggy wondered to herself if maybe her mother had not yet received the letter, because she hadn't said anything about it and here, she was making a dress as though travelling four hours by train was simply what a mother does when her daughter needed a new dress. Surely if she had received the letter, she would have been reluctant to hop on a train and travel all this way to spend her days bent over some silk and chiffon in another woman's home.

"Hi Mama. Hi Mrs. Penske. How are you old dears?" said Peggy, stopping to kiss her mother's pink cheek. She smiled when she realized that her mother had continued her old habit of poking a pencil through her chignon while she sewed. She had to remind herself that she had been living away from home for mere months, not the ages it sometimes felt like.

"Hello darling, how was work? Did you have any more of those interviews you have been telling

Daddy and me so much about?"

"No, today was a writing day. Today I spent the day in the office preparing a story about the women at Newsweek. It's impressive how many women work in their copy room, compared to other places." Peggy added a silent lament about how few women at the Tribune had ever made it to the copy room. She knew that she ought to be grateful that John had selected her, and she knew that she really was the best of the best, in her humble opinion, but it was still frustrating to be the exception rather than the rule.

"I'm just going to freshen up and I will be right back," said Peggy, noticing Rita in the hall.

"Hey there, Peggy Sue! How's tricks?" Rita wore one of her traditionally garish ensembles - pink patent leather ankle height boots, fluorescent purple pantyhose, a bright yellow minidress dotted with bright green flowers. Her hair was teased into a bouffant that made her about four inches taller than her natural height and she radiated happiness.

"Fine, thanks, Rita. How about you? You seem even more buoyant than usual."

"I had the most amazing day! Shirley Knight, the actress in The Sweet Bird of Youth, ya know? Well, she came into the shop today, and asked me, little ole me to help her pick out some clothes for a photo shoot that she's doin' next week! Can ya believe it? Clothes that I picked out are gonna be in

a magazine! A real, honest-to-goodness magazine!!!
I can't even explain how excitin' this is ta me!!!"

Peggy beamed at her friend. She did not know who
the actress was that Rita had styled, but that didn't
matter. What mattered was that Rita had styled
someone and that someone was going to be in a
magazine.

"Oh gosh, Rita! That is so amazing. I'm so happy
for you. Did she say which magazine, so we can all
get copies?"

"Screen Stars. I have even bought that magazine
before and now when I buy it, I will know that them
clothes on Shirley Knight were from my store and
that I picked 'em out!"

The two women walked up the steps one after the
other, headed to their rooms. Peggy gave Rita a
quick hug at the landing before heading up the
second flight to her attic bedroom. She unlocked
the door and walked into her sanctuary. She kicked
off her shoes and placed them to dry over the
heating vent by the closet, and carefully stripped off
her sweater, skirt and tights, folding each as she
went. There was something about having her
mother in the house that made her feel like she
ought to behave like a grown up. She pulled out her
favourite, worn old blue sweater, and a pair of
dungarees and changed quickly. She brushed her
tangle of auburn hair into a ponytail and tied it in

place. She chose to forgo freshening her makeup, instead rubbing some Vaseline on her lips and declaring herself perfect. She padded over to her window seat and dug around for her hidden notebook. Finding it, she settled against the cushions and began to write.

29

For three days, Mrs. Brennan, with the help of Mrs. Penske, trimmed, and sewed, occasionally dropping sewing needles and straight pins on the carpet, causing the women living in the house to ensure they never entered the drawing room barefoot. As the days passed the beautiful burnt orange material began to take shape into an elegant cocktail dress.

Knee length, with a simple ruffle at the hem, a ruched bodice with a strapless sweetheart neckline. As the dress began to take shape, Peggy felt herself growing more and more excited about the dinner party. The idea that she would be able to present herself to such important people would do wonders for her career, she was sure of it. She still saw herself as the one with the beautiful office, with the heavy ashtray and the window that looked out over Main Street. She knew that she had the talent, and all that she needed was the right opportunity to make herself known to the right people. She once considered how John would react when he saw her in her new dress but quickly shook her head and snuffed that nonsense from her mind. She had no use for such fancies. She was determined that she would not let silly thoughts of romance deter her from becoming the important journalist that she knew she was meant to be. Besides, surely, he would be bringing Eliza as his date. His thoughts towards Peggy were simply professional. He needed her to help him produce a competent, intelligent women's section for the Tribune and nothing more.

While her mother worked, Peggy shopped her friends' closets for appropriate shoes. She considered white pumps from Kate, and an elegant suede sandal from Em, but neither quite worked with the colour of the gown. She had just decided that she would simply have to make do with the black heels she had worn the night that John invited her to join the women's section, when Rita came to the rescue. Peggy had not thought to look to Rita, as her taste was so much more vibrant and bolder than her own, but here Rita appeared with a pair of gold strappy sandals, with a crystal-encrusted stiletto heel.

"Oh Rita, these are perfect! Are you sure I can borrow them?" Peggy gasped.

"Of course! Consider 'em yours... for the evenin'," Rita winked. Peggy smiled and kissed her friend's cheek.

"Thank you so much, Rita! These are perfect. You are a saint!"

On the last night of Mrs. Brennan's sojourn, she and Peggy were settled in the parlour while Mrs. Brennan hand sewed delicate beads to the bodice of the dress. Peggy had enjoyed having her mother staying in her home. It was such a comfort, and to have her dress made up in the perfect style for such an important occasion was more than Peggy had dreamed. She looked over at her mother, whose pink tongue was poking out through the corner of her teeth in concentration and decided to ask what had been on her mind for the past 4 days.

"Mother, are you happy?"

Mrs. Brennan turned to look at her daughter and sighed ever so slightly. "I was wondering when we would come to this. I was in the midst of replying to your letter when you called with the dress emergency and did not have time to finish. In answer to your question now – yes, I am happy. In response to your concerns in your letter, all that I have ever wanted for you, or for any of my children is that you are happy. It's true that your vision of happiness - becoming an intrepid journalist with her name in the paper - is not what I envisioned for you as a little girl, but that does not mean it is the wrong path, Margaret. When I was a young girl, I dreamed of being a concert pianist," said Mrs. Brennan, as Peggy watched her with surprise. "I adored the piano and dreamed of playing in big halls and auditoriums where people would come to hear me play. I would wear a fetching gown and be met with standing ovations." Mrs. Brennan chuckled and coloured ever so slightly at the memory of her girlhood fantasy.

"Well, Mother! What happened? I have not seen you so much as play the piano in years!"

"Like most women from my generation, I met your father, and we built a life together. When there are children running about, one does not have much time for piano playing. I suppose I ought to have kept it up, but between the washing, and the cooking, and the children, and the shopping, and the mending of clothing, there was just so little time left in the day, and I could hardly play the piano once everyone went to bed, as it would have woken you all up. So, the piano began to collect dust, and I am certain it is long out of tune now. All that is to say, while your sisters chose to marry and have traditional lives, well up until recently, at least, and that may have been what I had envisioned for you as a young girl, which does not mean that that is the only path that is right for you. I see you head off to work, and you are so proud of what you do. I hear your stories of interviews and writing and working with Caro and Mr. Grant, and I cannot help but be proud of the life that you have chosen for yourself. Do I miss you and wish you lived close to home with Daddy and me? Of course. But I wouldn't change a thing about your life, so long as you are happy and feel like you are where you want to be."

Peggy listened intently to her mother's words and saw now that when her mother was staring over the ironing at the Blue Mountains out of the kitchen window that perhaps she was not wishing she was elsewhere but rather hearing the distant sounds of a piano concert in her head. She could picture her mother sitting at the small piano in the living room, elegant fingers poised above the black and ivory keys, preparing to play a tune for the family, and she felt sad all over again that her mother had given up so much for her family. It made her strengthen her resolve that she would not give up on her goals. She would not find herself tied to laundry and babies and cooking. She would be a journalist who put her career first, and she would move ahead. She would not be trapped like Joanie or Linda. She would not feel the need to run away from her life like Linda had done. She would be important and proud and strong.

"Mother, have you heard from Linda? I am so worried about her, driving out west with her friend and no way for us to get in touch with her." Peggy watched her mother set the beadwork onto her lap and sigh again.

"I heard from her just before you called. She has made it to San Francisco and intends to stay with her friend. She has joined a group who are protesting the war, and she says she has found where she needs to be. She said that she will not be returning to Tom as long as Fred continues to live with them, and as Tom has made it clear that he would not be asking Fred to leave, she feels that their marriage is over. She intends to seek a divorce." Peggy's eyes widened as she listened to her mother. Lindy getting a divorce was unbelievable. It's true that she and Tom had no children, but for Lindy to join a protest movement and divorce her husband seemed so out of character that Peggy felt gob smacked.

"Protesting the war? Divorce? What do you make of it all?" Peggy had read about the protests in the paper, but she had never dreamed that her own sister might be among those who were angry at the government about the continued sending of troops to fight a war that they did not feel the government had any right in participating in.

"Honestly, Margaret, I don't know. But as I just said, my only dream for my children is that you are all happy. If Linda is happy being out west, and feels that she is doing good, there is not much that I can say. She is a grown woman now," said Mrs. Brennan as she resumed her needlework. Peggy slumped back into her seat and picked up the teacup resting on the table next to her elbow. She pictured Linda with her hair loose, wearing a peasant blouse and dungarees, holding a sign that said "Make Love Not War" as she had seen a young woman in the paper do recently and she thought about what must have caused such a dramatic shift in her older sister's behaviour. She could hear her saying "Daisy, this is what I was meant to do. People are dying and it needs to stop." Her sister had always had a soft heart and the desire to do things to make people happy. She could see this as a potential driving force to her sister's protesting, but the very act of protesting seemed so unlike her anti-confrontational nature that Peggy had a hard time reckoning the two images.

30

Peggy set her hair in curlers and applied delicate makeup to her face. She gave her lips a glossy cherry finish and slipped into the burnt orange cocktail dress that her mother had worked so tirelessly to create. The beading on the bodice added shimmer to the elegant ruching. She felt like she had stepped out of one of Rita's magazines. She stepped into Rita's gold heels and turned to face the mirror. The shade of her dress set of her auburn hair perfectly and she added a tiny gold heart necklace that her parents had given her for her 16th birthday. She reached for Kate's good wool coat and put it on over the soie de chine creation and picked up Emily's tiny gold clutch. She felt like Cinderella headed to the ball.

As she arrived at the Grant mansion, she double checked that she had her invitation and gave herself a peptalk. She told herself that she was invited, and in fact was expected to be there. She would be bubbly and warm and intelligent. She had read that morning's Tribune front to back, including the sports section so that she would be informed on any topic that was brought to the table. She knew that she looked the part of a young up and comer and that her gown could easily come from the racks of the finest shops in the city, but she still felt the old butterflies in her belly as she walked up the grand marble steps to the elegant front doors. Just as she was wondering whether to knock or simply walk in, the door opened, and John appeared in a formal black suit with a black bowtie. His sparkling blue eyes lit up when he saw her. Breaking into a grin, he said "Welcome, Peggy! I'm so glad you could make it." He ushered her into the foyer and offered to take her jacket.

"You look beautiful," he said, admiring her dress.

"Thank you," Peggy said with a smile. She didn't know whether it was appropriate to tell him that he looked handsome, so she decided it was best to say nothing at all. Though he did look dashing. She followed John through the foyer into the first door on the right and found herself in the midst of an enormous crowd of people standing under an equally enormous crystal chandelier. She gripped her clutch tighter, trying not to let her cheeks colour with nerves. She felt her ankle wobble slightly in her high heeled shoes and glanced quickly at John to see if he had noticed. He smiled at her warmly.

"Ready to meet some folks? Or would you like a drink first?" John asked, indicating towards a small bar near the sweeping windows. Peggy shook her head and said, "I am ready to meet people." She said a mental prayer that she does not slip on the shiny marble floor, as John led her further into the room. She recognized some of the men from the Board, standing alongside their glittering wives, and she noticed Caro holding forth in one corner. She was draped in a shimmering green chiffon gown, her hair pinned up on one side with a crystal barrette and was laughing loudly at something a man standing near her said.

Peggy could imagine herself in that scenario in a short time. She would be the one that everyone listened to when she spoke. She would confidently share stories about her journalistic endeavours. She would have real stories from the trenches, and she would be considered an expert worth listening to.

"Peggy, I'd like you to meet Peter Winthrop," said John as they stopped next to a group of people standing in the centre of the room. Peggy put out her hand to the redheaded man that John indicated. The man took her hand and instead of shaking it as she anticipated, he flipped her hand and kissed the back of it, like a courtly old gentleman. Peggy nearly gasped with surprise and annoyance. She was here to be taken seriously as a reporter at the Tribune, not to be treated like a prize princess.

"Peter, this is Peggy, a junior reporter for the women's section at the paper." Peggy thought that John might have saved her a little dignity by leaving off the 'junior', and she pursed her lips slightly. "Peggy, Peter works in the accounting department and is a longtime friend of the family."

"It's lovely to meet you, Peter," said Peggy with what she hoped was a winning smile, "how do you like accounting?" Peggy felt herself flush at the ridiculousness of the question. She wanted to be an ace reporter and the best opening question she could think of is 'how do you like accounting?'. John chuckled at her side and said "Pete is great with the books. We wouldn't trust them with anyone else."

"That's kind of you, John. I'm just happy to do my part and keep the good ol' Trib running smoothly." John patted Peter on the back, and turned to the blonde woman standing next to him, "hello, Jackie, how are the kids?" Jackie smiled and said they were fine, but at the stage where they get into everything. Peggy nodded along as though this were interesting information, all while scanning the room furtively for the next Important Person to be introduced to. She had already met Mr. Grant but felt that the more time that she spent getting to know him, the better her chances at moving up in the paper would be. She was not interested in hearing about children or the boring life of a young mother, but John seemed utterly fascinated by everything that Jackie had to say.

"How about you, Peggy?" asked Peter, "Do you have children?"

"No, I am working on my career. I don't have time for marriage or children," she answered in a slightly haughty tone. She noticed that John's bright blue eyes twinkled slightly as she spoke, nearly as though he were trying to repress one of his chuckles.

"Oh! You just haven't met the right one yet," laughed Peter, and Jackie smiled and nodded next to him, "Jackie here had thoughts of being a lawyer until we met. Now she is happy to be at home with Junie and Roger."

"I really couldn't be happier," smiled Jackie demurely.

Peggy suppressed a grimace. She had seen that and heard that hundreds of times from hundreds of people. The desire to reprove Jackie was almost more than Peggy could bear. She wanted to ask Mother to Junie and Roger what happened to Jackie the Lawyer with goals and dreams of her own. She wanted to know what was so great about Mr Overbearing Peter that he was worth them up. She did not understand how it was that women were expected to give everything up for love. Love of husband, love of children, love of home. Why couldn't she have love and love of career? The thought shocked her slightly, as the idea of her being in love was not something she had ever considered. As far as she was concerned, as far as she had ever been concerned love was to be avoided at all costs because the cost of love on her dreams was too great. Her byline beckoned to her, and she was all too certain that ending up with a man like Peter, or like the men her sisters had married would take her away from it. She couldn't bear the thought of giving it up when she was so close. She could almost feel the weight of her cut glass ashtray-to-be in her hand. She gripped her cocktail glass a little tighter. As she mentally rejoined the conversation, she gave a tight lip smile as Jackie described Junie's recent bout with the flu to a rapt John. She could not imagine why a man as intelligent and progressive as John would be so engaged with a woman who had given everything up to learn how much cough syrup was appropriate for a two-year-old. Peggy tried to catch John's eye, with the intention of telegraphing to him that perhaps they could move on and maybe even spend some time with his father before it came time to be seated for dinner, but he was focused on his clearly delightful conversation with Jackie and Peter. She took a small sip from her glass and glanced around the enormous room. Along the back wall, someone had opened the large oak doors which led to an equally spacious dining room, lined with long tables. Each table was set with elaborate centerpieces and from where Peggy stood it seemed that each seat had a place card. Her anxiety was piqued at the thought of being seated away from John and being left alone. She straightened up and set her chin. If she was to be alone at a table full of unfamiliar people, she would just do what she always did in that sort of situation – she would gladhand and introduce herself to everyone seated around her. Maybe she would be lucky, and they would turn out to be useful contacts for her to know.

"Peggy?" she heard John trying to get her attention. She flashed him her brightest smile, as he took her arm and asked "shall we head in? I see you noticed that they opened the doors for dinner." His eyes sparkled as he looked at her, and she felt her cheeks flush. He really was a very handsome man, she allowed, before reminding herself that he was her boss, and besides that, she had no interest in him like that, and besides that, even if she was interested, he was already involved with Eliza. She realized with a start that Eliza must be here somewhere. Suddenly she had even more reason for anxiety – what if she had to spend the whole evening listening to Eliza say "Jaaaawn" every thirty seconds. In a flash, Peggy gulped the remainder of her glass and set it on a nearby high top, before allowing John to take her arm.

"Thirsty?" John asked in an amused voice.

"No! I simply did not want to waste a perfectly good cocktail," Peggy blushed. She allowed herself to be led across the room and through the oak doors towards the long tables. She said a silent prayer that she would be seated near John and another one that they would be seated near his parents. She was about to ask about the seating arrangements when he suddenly dropped her arm and pulled out a chair indicating to her to have a seat. She glanced quickly at the place cards on either side of hers and felt a nervous flutter when neither belonged to John. As she sat, and attempted clumsily to pull in her own chair, she watched as John walked away towards the end of the table. She was just mustering her resolve when he reappeared across from her and sat down himself. Peggy allowed herself a small sigh of relief. She would be sitting with him after all. Now she looked at the names assigned to the seats next to her and tried to register if they were familiar. She did not recognize either one of them, but she dearly hoped that they would be of some great interest.

"Water?" asked a young waitress at her left elbow asked, holding a glass bottle wrapped in a white napkin. Peggy nodded politely and the woman poured into her water goblet. "Can I interest you in a glass of wine?"

Peggy asked for a glass of white wine and took a sip, not knowing how to pretend to know whether the wine was good or bad. It tasted fine to her, so she smiled and nodded at the woman to fill the glass.

Peggy looked over at John, who had ordered a glass of red wine. He seemed to know what to do with the sipping and the swilling and the tasting of his wine, and she tried not to feel annoyed that his upbringing had allowed him these social graces of which she had none. Her parents had not been sophisticated in the ways of wine, as far as she knew. Although perhaps her father, who enjoyed a scotch after work, may have known how to order wine when out with his important clients in the city every day. She would have to ask him one day if he could teach her. She wanted to seem just as worldly as John looked now and she wanted to feel at home in these situations.

"Will Eliza be here tonight?" Peggy blurted out to John as he turned to face her at the table. A look of confusion settled on to his face.

"Eliza? No, she won't be here tonight. This is for people related to the Tribune, and of course their spouses," he still looked bemused, and cocked his head to the right to examine her.

"Oh, I'm sorry, I just assumed that she would be here as your date," Peggy said, wondering what had come over her. In what land had she suddenly become the type of person who would say such a thing.

"My date? Peg, I invited you to come with me. So, I guess that would make you my 'date'," he said, running his hand over his dark hair. Peggy flushed crimson.

"Oh, well, ummm... ok," Peggy mumbled and tried to regain her composure, before rushing on "But aren't the two of you engaged? Should she not count as your spouse?"

John spat out his sip of wine with a guffaw, "ENGAGED?" he said, wiping his mouth with a napkin, "no, Eliza and I are most certainly not engaged. What on earth would make you say so?"

Peggy felt her face redden more, not having previously believed that it was possible to become any more embarrassed than she already felt. How had she been so wrong? She had her sights set on being an investigative journalist, and she couldn't even tell after all these months that Eliza and John were not engaged. What had made her believe that anyway? She had simply been so certain that they were that it never occurred to her to do any investigating or fact checking until tonight, in the beautiful dress that her mother had made for her. She didn't know if it was the dress or cocktail, she had drunk in one gulp that had made her so bold tonight as to ask about his relationship with Eliza but here she was and there was no way to back out of it now.

"I just thought that since you spent so much time together, and you are so friendly with each other that she was your fiancée. And your parents were so comfortable with her when I met them that it just seemed that naturally you were engaged..." Peggy petered out as she tried to explain where she had come to what was clearly an erroneous conclusion.

"No, Peggy, Eliza and I are not engaged. Nor have we ever been engaged. Nor will we ever become engaged. Eliza is engaged to my older brother, and he has never had an interest in the ol' Trib. He works in banking, and is therefore not here tonight, and so Eliza has no reason to be here, either" John spoke gently, as though he thought Peggy were made of glass. John was not going to marry Eliza. John was not engaged to her. This whole thing had been a figment of her imagination. She felt so foolish and quickly excused herself to find the lavatory. Once there she locked the door and looked in the mirror. Her cheeks were burning red, and her eyes looked fiercely green. Okay Peggy, she told herself. Get ahold of yourself, girl. She suddenly thought that maybe there could be more between her and John than simply coworkers, or boss and employee, because any inkling that she had had about that had always been shoved away, filed under the category of 'he is engaged to someone else'.

Was it possible that all those late-night conversations and after work drinks, and now this invitation for dinner meant more than she had allowed herself to think? Allowed herself to feel? She felt out of breath. Suddenly her beautiful burnt orange gown felt suffocating. She had a desperate desire to flee. To rip off her dress and curl up in the corner of her window seat. To stare out the window and sort through her thoughts. She wanted nothing more than to be completely and totally alone. But she could not do that. She had to be professional. She was being ridiculous. Of course, John was not thinking of her like this. He was a professional and besides, even if he wasn't engaged to Eliza, which did not mean he was available. And even if he was, she certainly did not want him! She was going to be Margaret Brennan, journalist, and that role would be all consuming. She would be like Caro and her whole world would be her writing. She slipped a cigarette from her purse and with shaking hands, lit it. She took a long drag and allowed a puff of smoke to escape her lips. She smoked until she felt her nerves settle and her hands stop shaking. She smoked until she could think clearly again, then she washed her hands, patted cool water on her cheeks and lifted her chin to her reflection. She marched back to the table and sat down just as the appetizer was being served.

John asked her quietly of she was alright, and she nodded curtly. She would not make a bigger fool of herself than she had already done this evening. She would not let this dress go to waste, and above all she would not waste this golden opportunity to meet the Right People who could help her with her career.

31

Peggy sat with her forehead against the bracingly cold window, watching the rain fall and swirl into puddles near the storm drain on the street. She had not gone to bed last night; in fact, she had not even taken the pins out of her now limply curled hair. Her dress lay in a crumpled heap on the floor just inside her locked door, where she had stepped out of it when she returned home, exhausted and worn out, but much too tired to sleep. She had slipped into her nightgown, wrapped herself in her housecoat, and slipped beneath the afghan on her window seat. She pulled out the little journal and began to write. Her loopy cursive covered pages upon pages as she worked through her feelings from the night before. She wrote of dancing and laughing and the people that she had met and shaken hands with. She wrote of the food they had eaten, the wine they had drunk, the cakes they had been served. And she wrote of John. How could it be that she had been so wrong? How was it possible that in all these months she had never asked him about Eliza? How had she allowed this to simply be a fact in her mind without any corroboration? Was it possible to work with John and also have feelings for him? No, of course not. She did not have feelings for him because she would never be like her mother. She would never stare longingly out the window while she ironed her husband's shirts and chased after snotty-nosed children all day long. She would never be on a first name basis with the butcher. She would never have dinner on the table for anyone but herself. She would dine on a cold can of beans, straight out of the can if that is what she felt like, and no one would be there to complain. She would sit barefoot and cross-legged on the floor of her own apartment piecing together her own articles and doing research for her own stories. She would order Chinese food from the place on the corner and eat it sitting on her own couch. She would never sit down to dinner at exactly 6 o'clock, because that was not her dream. She would be chasing leads and sitting on dark benches meeting with sources at all hours of the night. She would be tapping the ash off of her own cigarettes in her own office well into the wee hours of the morning. That was her life. There was not a single space left for a man to make himself at home. There was no way that she would ever let anyone slow her down. So why, as the cold winter morning light broke through the branches of the tree out her window, did she find herself thinking of John again, and again?

She heard Mrs. Penske walk down the hall past her room, headed for the kitchen, no doubt, to drink her first cup of coffee and begin to prepare breakfast for her charges. At the thought of food, Peggy realized that she was both hungry and exhausted. The high of the night before had finally worn off. Writing had sated her busy mind, and she was ready to tumble into bed and sleep for at least the next four hours. She pulled her curtains closed, so only the sliver of light would pass between the drapes, and padded across the room in her cold, bare feet. She picked up her dress, and after shaking out any wrinkles, she hung it in her wardrobe. Then she climbed into her chilly bed, pulling the comforter up to her chin, she rolled over, so she faced away from the window's light and fell into an immediate and very deep sleep.

32

Peggy tried to smooth the frizz from her wet hair in the ladies' room at The Tribune office, before she made her way to her desk, no longer in the typing pool but right outside John's office. Caro's office was across the hall from John's and six small desks made up the space between, one of which was Peggy's. She had just enough room for her typewriter, her small silver ashtray, a coffee cup and a blotter. If she needed any more space than that, she had to make the trek to the conference room at the end of the hall to spread out the pieces that she was working on for the Women's pages. The hem of her corduroy skirt was wet with rain and her boots looked sodden. She felt that she looked an absolute fright, but there wasn't anything she could do about it now. She had been caught in a torrential downpour on her way to the office, and her disdain for umbrellas meant that she always went without one. On her way to her desk, she stopped and filled a paper cup with the office's terrible coffee. It may be thick and bitter, but at least it would warm her up from the inside. She carried her cup and winced as she heard her shoes slosh on the floor all the way to her desk. Setting the paper cup on the desk, she went and hung her sopping coat on the coat rack in the corner where it would spend the day drip, dripping on to the floor, until it was time to be worn home, cold and sticky.

"Peggy?" she heard John call from inside his office. She picked up her pen and notebook and headed towards his voice.

"Yes?" she asked, poking her auburn head around the door frame. He was sitting behind his large desk; his forelock clicked back with Brylcreem. He was already smoking, which told her it was going to be a very busy day. He did not usually have his first cigarette until lunch, so for him to be smoking at 8 o'clock, she knew they were going to hit the ground running.

He glanced up at her and smiled, "Ever considered an umbrella, kid?" It was a running joke between them – he never went anywhere without an umbrella, and she would rather be caught in a rain storm than be encumbered by one. Today, she was just so lucky.

"You know me. Umbrellas aren't my thing. It's hard enough getting around town with my wits about me, let alone doing it with a purse and an umbrella. You'll just have to put up with me looking like a drowned rat for the day."

He smiled again, "You hardly look like a rat, Peg." She loved it when he called her Peg. It felt like his own term of endearment, even though many of her friends called her by the nickname. Maybe that was what made it feel so special – it made them feel like friends, rather than boss and employee. She sat down in one of the armchairs facing his desk, perched on the edge of the seat, pen poised over her notebook, ready for whatever John had called her into his office for.

"I need you to go with Caro this afternoon to interview Mavis Brinkley. She will do the actual interview, but I think it would be good for you to be there, to get an idea how these things go, so you can eventually take on interviewing subjects yourself." Any affection that Peggy had felt moments ago was replaced with a white-hot irritation at the idea of her needing to be trained on interviewing. She had interviewed people at her school paper. Sure, Mavis Brinkley was an important woman, but surely it couldn't be that difficult or that different from the interviews that she had done in the past. It annoyed her to no end when John thought that she needed guidance from Caro, or anyone else for that matter. She was a talented writer and was determined that people should know that without her having to prove herself. She knew she could write and probably interview just as well as Caro. Maybe even better. She chose to bite her tongue and nodded quietly as John spoke. She knew that if he was already smoking, it was not the time to push back against him. There would certainly be time for that. Or better yet, maybe Caro would allow her to do the interview and then she would tell John what a wonderful job she had done, and then Peggy would not have to say anything, and she would certainly be handed choice interviews going forward.

"And after you both come back," John was saying, taking another puff on his cigarette, "we will be having a content meeting. It will likely run late, so please have Mrs. Kelly order dinner for everyone. I think something from the deli downstairs should suffice, but I'd rather make sure we get fed before it closes for the night."

Peggy nodded and prepared to stand to go give Mrs. Kelly her marching orders when he stopped her and said "please borrow my umbrella for the interview. It would hardly do for you to drip all over Mrs. Brinkley's famously white sofas." He winked at her as she made her way to the door. It suddenly occurred to her that she was going to meet a famous writer this afternoon, and all of her hair was standing on end from being wet. She simply despised her hair on days like this. There was nothing she could do about it now. She could hardly go home, wash her hair, and re-set it in this weather. The frizz would do what it wanted regardless. Maybe she could sneak across to the chemist and buy some Aqua Net and make something of whatever this mess could be. That seemed to be the easiest solution and the only option available to her at this point. She quickly gave Mrs. Kelly the request for a simple deli dinner before grabbing her coat from where it continued to drip noiselessly onto the floor and rushed downstairs with her purse to buy the hairspray that she hoped would save the day.

Peggy sat perched on the edge of one of Mavis Brinkley's white sofas, watching Caro conduct her interview. She thought that she would have done just as well as Caro in interviewing Mrs. Brinkley, had she been entrusted with the task herself. She resented that John thought that she needed to be trained in the art of interviewing. How hard could it possibly be? It was no different interviewing a famous writer than it had been interviewing classmates and professors at school. She daintily took a sip of tea from the tiny teacup on the table in front of her and pretended to be paying rapt attention to the conversation between Caro and Mrs. Brinkley. In truth, she was imagining her own future, when she would be the one doing the interviewing. Or even better, when she was so well regarded that she would be the one being interviewed. She could picture herself sitting in a room at least as well-appointed as this one and she would be wearing the most glamorous of dresses, while important journalists asked her what the secret to her stunning success was. She would smile coyly and refuse to share too much but would offer little tidbits that would make excellent pull quotes for their article about her. As Caro wrapped the interview up, Mrs. Brinkley handed each of the women a signed copy of her newest book. The gift sent a little thrill through Peggy, as she had never received a signed book from an author before. She imagined that if she ever wrote a book instead of pursuing journalism, she would keep a stack on hand to give to anyone who came to visit her. The idea of a little stack of books with her name on the spine made her smile. She thanked Mrs. Brinkley sincerely and followed Caro out of the beautiful apartment. On the drive back to the Tribune offices she peppered Caro with questions. Why had she worded such question in this way? How had she prepared for the interview? Most importantly, she felt, how can she convince John that she is ready for interviews herself.

"First of all," said Caro, "You need to slow down. Grant will assign you interviews that he thinks you are ready for as you are ready for them. You can't rush your training process. Secondly, you need to remember that the more training you have the better prepared you will be for your first solo interview."

"But I have performed interviews before! At college, for the school paper, I interviewed students and professors all of the time. I think he is being too concerned by not letting me interview people yet. I mean, I did the intake interviews at the diner when we were first getting set up. How is this different?"

"The fact that you need to ask how interviewing Mavis Brinkley is different than interviewing students for a school paper is exactly why Grant has you shadowing me," laughed Caro with a flip of her bobbed hair. Peggy watched as Caro tapped her long, red polished nail on the top of the steering wheel while they waited at a stop light. Caro was the only person that Peggy had met since coming to the city who owned a car. Caro claimed it was, so she did not have to wait for a taxi or the train to get to her meetings, but Peggy secretly wondered if it was a status symbol. Proof of just how far the only female reporter at the Tribune had really made it, right there in the robin's egg blue steel. Peggy didn't think that a car was the purchase that she would make once she had that corner office with the view of the park and the cut glass ash tray. She thought she would much rather invest in a nice apartment full of beautiful things, like vases always full of fresh flowers and bookcases stacked full of books and tchotchkes. In all fairness, Peggy allowed, maybe Caro also had a beautiful apartment with fancy art and closets teeming with beautiful clothes. She had never seen Caro's home, nor had she asked about it.

Caro seemed to take Peggy's silence as sullenness and began again. "Listen, I am happy to show you the ropes, kid. You just must be willing to pace yourself. None of us made it overnight, and none of us is a journalistic prodigy. Let Grant get you trained up and then when you are ready, you will know."

"How did you know when you were ready?" sighed Peggy, resolved to get through her training phase twice as quickly as any man on the paper had.

"I can tell you that I wasn't ready during my first 10 interviews! I ummmed and ahhhhed and said 'that's lovely' to every statement made. I did not know what questions to ask, and I blasted through the ones I had prepared much more quickly than I expected to. Overall, I was an absolute mess for the first year that I had this job. I am lucky that I picked up quicker than most, though, or I would have been out pounding the pavement looking for a new job quicker than you can say Jack Robinson."

A year! And that was considered quicker than most? No, surely not. Peggy picked at an invisible piece of lint on her corduroy skirt and resolved to beat Caro's year by at least 6 months. Maybe even more. There was no way it would take her a year to be comfortable asking people questions. She asked questions all of the time.

"One more thing, Peggy," Caro said, "I've seen the way that you and Grant look at each other. If you want to be taken seriously at the paper, you can't be making moon eyes at the editor."

Peggy was shocked. She had never made 'moon eyes' at anyone, and she was hardly going to start with John. She knew how important it was to succeed as a journalist on her own merit. It was true that since discovering that John and Eliza were not engaged, she had found herself noticing him more and reading more into the words that they exchanged. It was true, but she could not believe that Caro would bring this up to her. How had she even noticed when Peggy herself did not notice.

"I surely do not know what you mean by that!" exclaimed Peggy, cheeks reddening, chin tipping defiantly. She felt angry tears well in her eyes. Why must she become teary when mad? It was such a little girl thing to do, and she was not a little girl.

"If you say so, kiddo. Just don't say I didn't warn you if things go sideways," said Caro in a slightly ominous, though mocking tone.

Peggy thought about Caro's words. She had said how John and she looked at each other. Did that mean that John looked at her in a certain way? How did he look at her? What had she missed over all their meetings and appointments? She considered herself a keen judge of character and extraordinarily perceptive, so what did it say if John had been looking at her in a certain way and she had not noticed. And in her heart of hearts, she wondered if maybe she had noticed and simply pushed those thoughts aside.

34

Dinner was always a raucous affair when she was home to eat. All the girls vying for a place at the table, passing food around family-style, gossiping and chatting about their days. Mrs. Penske and her daughter were exquisite cooks, and the girls all knew how lucky they were to have the board part of their room and board be so delicious. Tonight, Peggy followed her nose to find a standing rib roast, mashed potatoes, buttered peas, and fresh dinner rolls, with a succulent brown gravy. She filled her wine goblet and brought it to the table, settling in between Em and Kate. She sat back in her seat and allowed the cacophony to wash over her, mingling with the scent of the meal to come. Kate was talking about how the children she nannied had behaved that day, and how grateful she was for an evening off. Emily was listening quietly as Rita described a date she had been on the night before. Emily was still hurting from the loss of her relationship with Teddy, but she had reached a point where she could listen to the other girls talk about their dates without welling up with tears.

"I tell ya, Em, he just up and paid the bill while I was in the ladies. No going Dutch this time. He really is an awful swell guy; he just doesn't get that a gal likes to pay her own way. I don't need him thinkin' I owe him anythin'".

Rita was speaking animatedly with her multi-ringed fingers flying through the air. Emily shook her head slightly.

"Rita, if the poor man wants to pay, let him. He has to prove that he is worth your time, and maybe this is how he wants to do it. Why when Teddy and I were dating, if he didn't pay for our meals, no one was going to." She cast her eyes down at the mention of Teddy, but that was the only sign of hurt that his name caused her.

Peggy took a sip of her wine and let the sour tang of it wash over her tongue. She was not a wine connoisseur by any stretch of the imagination, but she enjoyed it now and again. It made her feel grown up to sip the warm red liquid and feel it warm her from the inside. If only it did not make her cheeks so hot, she felt she could enjoy it more.

"Pass the peas," said Audrey, nodding to the steaming bowl in front of Peggy. She helped herself to a scoopful and then passed the dish to Kate who passed it to Audrey.

"How about you, Peggy Sue?" said Rita, "anyone strike your fancy at that ol' newspaper of yours?" Rita was constantly hoping that Peggy would fall in love with a famous journalist, and they would become The It Couple of the news industry.

"No. As I have said a million times before, I am not interested in love. I want to be a serious journalist, and I can't do that if I am all... all...

twitterpated! John says that I have what it takes to get ahead, and he says that if I stay focused I will definitely get my byline." Now John had never strictly said this, but it was what Peggy believed, nonetheless, and she knew that that would be the advice that John would give her if she ever asked for his advice.

"He is the one engaged to the shopgirl, right?" asked Emily politely. Peggy squirmed uncomfortably in her seat. She had told Emily about her assumption as though it had been fact and now she felt as embarrassed as if she had to print a retraction in the paper.

"Well, not strictly speaking. It turns out that it is his brother, who works in banking, who is engaged to Eliza. They have known each other their whole lives, which is why they are so chummy when they see each other. But it turns out that John is not, in fact, engaged to anyone, at the moment."

"At the moment? Had he been engaged before?" asked Kate with genuine curiosity.

"Um, well, no. At least not as far as I know he has not been," Peggy reddened and took a larger sip from her glass, before reaching for the bowl of piping hot mashed potatoes. She hoped desperately that the girls would move on, she did not want to discuss John anymore. Ever since her conversation

with Caro in the car, she felt awkward and
wrongfooted when it came to him. She did not want
to lead him on to thinking that she was interested,
when she had always been perfectly clear with her
ambitions. Career above all else. Career before
love. Career before family. Career, career, career. It
was true that in the darkest recesses of her heart she
fantasized about having both – a career and a
supportive husband who understood how important
her career was to her. A man who knew that she
would always be Margaret Anne Brennan, journalist
and she would always want to investigate and chase
the stories and was ok with coming home to dinner
not on the stove. In fact, a man who would meet
her for a grilled cheese sandwich at the diner rather
than expect a home cooked meal. That was her
dream. But she knew that that was just not how it
worked. She would be expected to marry, settle
down, keep house, raise babies and never write
more than a cheque for the butcher for the rest of
her life. She just could not take that risk. She
needed her byline; she had worked too hard to get
where she was and she had no desire to give up until
it came true.

"Peg, maybe that's what you need. A man who
works in the same sort of job that you do. A man
who understands the effort that you put into your
career and also wants one of his own. Maybe John
might be the man for you," said Emily quietly, but
with conviction.

Peggy dug into her mashed potatoes. She could not be expected to respond with her mouth full, so her goal for the remainder of the meal was to have her mouth filled at all times. She knew that even if John saw the importance of women's pages at the Tribune that did not mean he would not want his wife to be the type who could cook a roast and darn a sock. Working in journalism, he was more likely to need the type of wife that would manage the home so he could go out and make his name for himself. She could not be the type of wife that she assumed he would need. She could not be any type of wife. She could just be herself, and that meant that she could not, would not even imagine a married life.

35

She sat in the sunlight, sipping her paper cup of coffee. It was the first sunny day in weeks and Peggy was determined to enjoy it, regardless of the cold. Her hands were wrapped warmly in her cozy gloves, and she wore her knitted hat pulled down over her ears, just the way her mother would have insisted that she wear it. She wished that she could wear pants to work as a shiver went down her spine, in her warmest dress. Even in woolen stockings her legs felt the chill. She turned her face towards the sun and closed her eyes, trying to soak up any particles of warmth to be found.

"What are you doing down here?" came a disembodied voice. Peggy looked and found herself facing John, who had that same amused twinkle in his eye. His forelock fell down into his face below his hat which had clearly been placed in a hurry. He was still buttoning the top button of his winter coat, as though he had left his office in a rush. He motioned to the spot next to her on the bench, silently asking to join her. She patted the seat next to her and he sat.

"I came down for some sunshine on my lunch break. I haven't missed my time, have I?" she asked quickly moving to check her wristwatch.

"No, no. Not at all. I was just looking for you and I

did not imagine I would find you so close to the office, basking in the sunshine, on this frosty day."

"Why?"

"Because it is cold out. Who

would want to sit outside and

catch a chill?" "No, why

were you looking for me?"

"Oh. Because I need you to write a piece and I need you to write it today. Mr. Forster has cut the section on the women's coalition and wants something more fashion-forward." John seemed almost on edge as he told Peggy his reasoning for hunting her down.

"What was wrong with the women's coalition piece? Why do we need more fashion? We are already doing that segment on Rudolph Nagaya and his new store opening downtown. Isn't that enough fashion for one week?" Peggy was indignant, not because she had written the piece, it had been one of Caro's, but because she felt that women in politics was a lot more critical to women reading the women's pages than another feature on pantyhose.

"He said that there is already too much about politics in Sunday's paper, so we need to even it out and make it more accessible to women. Do you have an idea for a piece? I am thinking if we can come up with something creative, we might even be able to get you a byline on this one." Peggy sat up straighter. Usually, any copy that she wrote was written and published with no byline, simply as an article in the Tribune and labelled "staff reporter", as was the policy for unknown writers. The idea of finally having her own byline made the anger at the last-minute pulling of the coalition piece subside slightly. She decided that maybe she could make a fashion-related piece, but also make it political, thinking of her discomfort at wearing a dress and skirts in the cold weather.

"What about a piece on workplace dress codes that penalize women and allow men to wear nearly anything that they want on any given day?"

"Penalizes women? What dress code does that?" John asked, genuinely confused. Peggy rolled her eyes.

"Look at what you are wearing against the weather and look at what I am wearing. Your wool slacks are infinitely warmer and more comfortable than my stockings, yet it is unacceptable for me to wear pants to the office. It is unacceptable for me to have my shoulders showing on a hot day. It is unacceptable for me to wear a shirt without a collar. It is unacceptable to wear a skirt that shows my knees. It is unacceptable for me to wear shoes with less than a one-inch heel. It is unacceptable for me to wear open toed shoes. The list goes on and on, while you wear a nice warm suit in the winter, and a nice summer suit in the summer. You can take off your jacket and roll up your sleeves, and no one blanches at the sight of your forearms. It's a double standard, and I know the Trib is not the only workplace that has these rules. What if we wrote a piece about how women are being held to an unfair standard at work, while men are allowed to wear what they want, when they want?"

John examined her stocking-clad legs, then looked at her sincere face. He smiled and said "Well, it's not like we can wear whatever we like. We must wear a shirt and tie at all times, but I get your meaning.
Sure. If you think you can get enough information about that for a piece today, and it can't just be solely based on your own experience with dress codes, it has to be balanced, then I approve that story."

Peggy bolted to her feet and began to walk back to the big glass doors to the lobby of the Tribune, when John caught her hand and said, "but if you don't think you can write a balanced story, with facts about dress codes from other companies and workplaces, you will need to write a piece on next season's hats, or something equally simple to create by tonight's deadline. This needs to get to the editing team by eleven o'clock."

Peggy felt a warmth in her chest and a tingle in her hand where John held it. He had never touched her in such a way before and she was not keen to pull her hand away. She looked down into his beautiful blue eyes and felt a momentary connection. After what felt like an eternity and also only seconds, he dropped her hand as she nodded silently.

He stood and looked down at her, the sunlight a halo around her auburn hair and she wondered not for the first time what he was thinking. They turned and walked quietly back into the bustling lobby, where Peggy's heeled shoes made a clac-clac-clac sound as they approached the large elevator bank.

Peggy hung up the phone in the conference room, furiously scribbling notes into her Filofax. She crossed another company name off her list and proceeded to look for the next name she had written down and searched the yellow pages for the number. Her modus operandi for developing her first (potentially) bylined article was to find names of other companies where she had noted discrepancies between the way that men dressed and women, if they worked in the organizations at all, dressed. She covered the gamut from coffee shops, to libraries, to her own experience at the Tribune. So far, she had spoken to 15 women, five of whom were quick to say that there was nothing unfair about their company's dress code for reasons stemming from 'men can't help themselves if they see a shoulder', to 'it's for our own good. We wouldn't know how to dress professionally without a dress code', to 'that's just the way that it is. Why rock the boat?', but the other 10 were helpful and provided detailed practices that can be defined as nothing less than discriminatory. One woman even offered to hand deliver her employee handbook, if Peggy swore that she would never say where she got it from. This made Peggy thrilled for she had never had an anonymous source before. Peggy made notes and decided that she would use

the five women who did not see this as a problem
as the 'balance' John had insisted on. She looked at
the tiny gold numberless wristwatch and saw that it
was already a quarter past eight in the evening. She
checked her list and decided that she was not likely
to get ahold of anyone else, unless they worked in a
restaurant at this hour, and besides she really had to
start writing in order to make the 11 o'clock
deadline. She knew that John would want at least an
hour with it before it got sent over to the editing
department, so she quickly gathered up all of her
notes and pens and raced back to her desk.

The sun hadn't even risen, and Peggy was pacing the entryway in her bare feet, with her beloved afghan wrapped around her shoulders. She knew the paper would be delivered soon, and she wanted to be the first person to read it. No, she wanted to find her byline before anyone else looked at the paper. She knew that her piece was supposed to be in today's Women's section. She was really proud of the article she had written and was anxious to see it in print, under her very own name. John had told her that he was pleased with what she had written and he thought Mr. Forster would let it through, even though it wasn't about hats or handbags. Even with that, she still had a small niggling fear that it would be cut, or that her byline would be missing. She peeked through the window next to the front door for probably the fiftieth time that morning, checking for the paper boy.

"You are up early, dear," said Mrs. Penske quietly as she trudged down the stairs, smoothing back her hair.

"I'm just waiting for the paper. I wrote a piece and for the first time, my name is supposed to appear in print, and I am just anxious to see it," Peggy whispered conspiratorially. Mrs. Penske reached out and rubbed Peggy's shoulder and smiled.

"I will go make some coffee and we can wait together in the parlour where it is warm."

"Thank you, Mrs. P. Coffee would be wonderful." Peggy peeked one more time out the window and then wandered into the parlour and settled in the corner of the sofa, tucking her feet under the afghan and listening for any noise from the street.

All she could hear was Mrs. Penske preparing the coffee in the kitchen. She leaned her head against the back of the sofa and imagined opening the paper and scanning the women's section for her name. She wanted to see it so badly that it made her feel anxious. What if it had been cut? What if Mr. Forster was not okay with her dress code angle? What if he was offended by the idea that women might wear pants to work?

"Here you are, dear," Mrs. Penske said as she handed Peggy a cup of steaming coffee, softened with cream and sugar, just the way Peggy liked it. She took the cup and inhaled the rich aroma, before taking a sip.

Mrs. Penske sat down at the other end of the sofa and patted Peggy's knee, before sipping her own coffee. Peggy thought how nice it was that Mrs. Penske was waiting with her, because she knew that the older woman woke early each day to begin preparing breakfast for her house full of girls, and she would likely be doing that now, if Peggy were still in bed where she belonged.

They sat in companionable silence, drinking their coffee and watching the light begin to appear out the front window. 'Red sky in the morning, sailors take warning' she thought as the light began to turn the sky a brilliant crimson. Suddenly there was a soft thud at the front door and Peggy hastily set her cup on the table, forgetting to place it on a coaster, and dove for the front door. Sunday's thick paper lay haphazardly on the mat, and Peggy snatched it up before racing back to the parlour and plunging to the floor. She quickly untied the paper and spread it out in front of herself. She flipped hurriedly to the women's section and then slowed down. She scanned the first page, knowing that it would not be there, as the interview with Mrs. Brinkley was their feature of the week, but not wanting to miss it, nonetheless. She gingerly turned the page and continued to scan the headlines looking for the one she knew they had selected for her piece. She flipped through three pages and was beginning to lose hope that she had made it into this week's paper, when suddenly there it was. "The Way She Must Dress Has Her in Distress" by Margaret Anne Brennan. She sat back on her heels and took a deep breath. It was there. Her very first byline. Her name was in the Tribune. She was officially a journalist for the largest newspaper in the city and she had made it. Her hard work had paid off and this morning, people all across the city would be reading what she wrote while they ate their breakfasts.

"Well, dear? Is it there? Are you in the paper?"
asked Mrs. Penske gently. Peggy looked up at her
with tears in her eyes and could do nothing more
than nod. She pointed to her name and Mrs.
Penske let out a whoop of excitement, regardless
the fact that it was not yet 6 o'clock in the morning
and the house full of women were still sound asleep.
She knelt down on the carpet next to Peggy and
immediately began to read. Peggy could not believe
it. And yet. And yet she knew deep in her bones
that this is what she was meant to do. She knew that
she was a talented writer and a hard worker. She
knew that this piece was well written and given the
time constraints of having just one day, it was well
researched, too. She felt so proud of herself and
could not wait to share this with her family back
home. As soon as it was decent, she would call the
Brennan residence and let her parents know. She
also decided that she would visit the new agent
before breakfast and purchase a few more copies
for friends and family that lived outside of the
Tribune's delivery zone. She knew her sisters would
be so proud of her. She wished she knew where
Linda was so that she could send a copy to her as
well, but since that initial letter, Peggy had heard
nothing from her beloved older sister. It worried
her, that Lindy was on the west coast with no one to
turn to. She decided she would buy one for Linda
and would hold on to it until she had an address for
her, where she could write her and include the
clipping. She could picture her beautiful, blonde

sister reading the piece and thinking that her Daisy had made it. The thought filled Peggy with more pride and a twinge of joy.

"Well, I don't know that girls need to start wearing slacks to work, but that was a very good article, dear! I am going to cut it out and we can hang it in the hall so everyone can see how talented you are. I am mighty proud. Mighty proud, indeed." Mrs. Penske rose to her feet haltingly and turned towards the kitchen to begin preparing breakfast.

Peggy ran her finger over her name, as though she could feel it in raised ink. Margaret Anne Brennan. She had made it.

Peggy was proudly carrying a stack of newspapers back from the news agent's when it started to snow. She closed her eyes and smiled. Today was absolutely perfect. She had finally earned a byline in the paper, and now she was walking through silently dancing flakes. She walked along the quiet sidewalk, arms laden with papers, and imagining the reactions of her family back home when they tore open a letter from her, only to find that her dream had come true. She was not even sure how her parents would react, but she knew that in their heart of hearts they would be proud of her. She could imagine her mother pasting the clipping neatly into the family photo album, and she could see her father bringing the clipping to the office to share with his colleagues that his little girl was a journalist with the city's biggest paper. She imagined her brothers telling their families about Peggy's great success. She felt like all of her daring and hard work had paid off. She knew that she had more to do to get that office with the window, but she could not help being pleased with what she had accomplished so far.

She climbed the steps to the door of the boarding house and quietly let herself in. She stopped in the kitchen to borrow a pair of scissors from Mrs. Penske and then climbed the stairs to her little bedroom. She kicked off her snow dampened boots, dropped the newspapers in a pile to the floor, and tossed her coat on to her bed. She knew she would regret throwing a damp coat on her bed when it came time for sleep, but at the moment she had more important things to think about. She flopped down onto her belly on the rag rug next to her bed and drew the stack of newspapers to her. She flipped carelessly through them, one at a time, until she found her article and carefully, meticulously she cut the piece out of each one. When she was finished she had more than a dozen clippings and she set about writing letters to go with each article for each member of her family. She decided to send Linda's care of her mother, on the off chance Linda let her mother know where she was living out west. She still held out hope for another letter from her sister. They had always been so close, and she missed answering the phone to hear "Hello Daisy, dear." No one else called her Daisy, not that she would have let them, but it made her miss her sister all the more.

She wrote a letter to her mother and father and inserted two clippings into the envelope. She was certain they would each want a copy and that the idea of them sharing one clipping was simply preposterous. She wrote a letter to Joan, and George and Harry, and sent them each a clipping of the article. She wrote a letter to Lindy, she wrote a letter to her grandparents, although she knew that they would be shocked by the topic and would likely write her back to express their displeasure at the unladylike behaviour of young women. She wrote a note for Mrs. Tate and sealed it into an envelope to drop off at her shop that afternoon.

She found herself wondering if John was reading the paper this morning. She imagined him sitting at his breakfast table, with a hot cup of coffee in one hand and her article in the other. She imagined him smiling in that understated way of his. She knew he had already read the article days ago, but she imagined him feeling a sense of pride in her accomplishment. She had a dreamy look on her pale face when Kate walked into the room. "What are you doing?" Kate asked as she picked up

one of the many newspapers spread around Peggy.

"It's finally happened, Katie! I have a byline!"

Peggy grabbed the nearest clipping and thrust it toward her friend, who gently took it, as though it was a fragile item that might break if grasped too heartily.

"Oh, Peg! Really? I'm so happy for you! That's just what you have been working towards!"

Peggy grinned with pink blossoming across her cheeks. She didn't need to tell Kate that she really still wanted that office with the window overlooking the park and the heavy, cut-glass ash tray on her desk. She was just pleased that her friend was proud of her and recognised her accomplishment.

"Yep! I am just cutting out clippings to send home. I have a few leftover if you..." Peggy trailed off, almost sheepishly.

"Can I? Oh, I would love a copy. Your first byline. How exciting!" Kate quickly kissed Peggy on the cheek and gave her shoulder a squeeze before heading out to start her day.

Peggy smoothed out the clipping in front of her and marveled once again at her name – Margaret Brennan – written in bold, black type at the top of the page, just beneath the headline. She felt so proud and wished, not for the first time, that it was a Monday and that she could head into the office and see John. She shook her head, to rid herself of the silly, girlish thought. She did not need to see John. He had seen the article. He had approved the thing. She needed to stay focused. Having thoughts about John would not bring her any closer to that office, or that ashtray. This was the first step in what would certainly be a long and illustrious career, as a journalist. She pictured herself in Caro's shoes – interviewing important people, driving a lovely car. All in all, she decided, she ought to be thinking about her future, and just like when she was a young girl, she knew that that future did not hold room for marriage. Once a girl was married, she was expected to give up any notion of working and go home to live the life of a brood mare. That would not be her, so she had best leave that silliness behind her and focus on the future.

Stepping over the threshold of Mrs. Tate's little shop, Peggy felt the old woman's energy before she saw her. In every case, and messy stack, Peggy could sense Mrs. Tate's love for the store. The store that had once belonged to her husband was now thoroughly and undoubtably the purview of the tiny, blue haired woman.

"Mrs. Tate?" Peggy called into the store.

"Oh, Peggy! How nice to see you my dear! What can I help you find? Surely you can't need another notepad already! You just bought the last 3 that I had two days ago," Mrs. Tate's rheumy eyes sparkled as she looked up at the young woman standing before her. Dressed in a floral shift and a dusty apron, Mrs. Tate looked every bit the part of the funny old shopkeeper.

"No, no, not at all. I still have the notebooks. I am here to drop something off for you," Peggy said, sliding the little white envelope from her pocket and presenting it to Mrs. Tate. The old woman took the envelope and made to open it, then paused.

"May I open it now?" Mrs. Tate asked politely, her somewhat gnarled fingers itching to rip it open. Peggy smiled and nodded vigorously, a curl of auburn hair falling from behind her ear.

Mrs. Tate squealed like a child when she pulled out the clipping and saw Peggy's name, and nearly toppled the younger woman when she threw her arms around Peggy to give her a hug.

"Peggy, my girl! I am so proud of you! Has your mother seen this yet? I am absolutely positively sure this will make her cry," said Mrs. Tate with a wink, referring to when Peggy had confessed that she had never made her mother cry before.

"No, I am just on my way to mail these to my family, but I wanted to stop in and give you one right away. You have become family to me, Mrs. Tate, and I needed you to be one of the first to see it." Peggy blushed as she spoke and tucked the errant curl back into its place.

After agreeing to meet for coffee the following week, Peggy left the shop and walked down the sidewalk on the beautiful day. She tipped her face towards the sun, and closed her eyes, drinking in the warmth. She felt absolutely content in that moment, the feeling radiating from her chest, and settling like a smile on her face. She opened her eyes after a moment and began to walk towards the large red mailbox. She observed a man walking his dog, or rather, she thought to herself with a laugh, the dog walking the man, as the large brown dog pulled at his leash; she observed a young mother pushing a pram with an equally young man walking, with his hand lightly brushing her lower back. They looked happy, this couple with their baby. Peggy watched them stroll by and wondered what it was like at home. Would Little Mother be truly happy washing loads of dirty laundry all day, and vacuuming the rug, while Baby played on the floor? Would Little Father come home at the end of a long workday and bounce baby on his knee? Or would Little Mother do like her mother had, and gaze longingly at the life that she didn't have, and Little

Father would come home and expect dinner on the table like her father had? Peggy mused as she continued towards the mailbox.

Pulling the large red handle, Peggy opened the great red maw and pulled her stack of envelopes from her handbag. She carefully slid the stack inside and closed the mailbox, opening it just once to see that all the envelopes had fallen into the box; a habit her mother had taught her as a child sending letters to Santa.

Having completed her errands for the day, Peggy wandered aimlessly on the warm day, enjoying the sunlight and the breeze. She lit a cigarette as she walked, feeling ever so grown up; every inch the Margaret Brennan who had just hours ago been introduced to the world through her article in The Tribune. She continued down the street, passing shop windows and admiring her reflection as she did. She had to admit that she felt confident this morning, in her purple and brown floral A-line skirt, and light cotton blouse, her curls tumbling freely and haphazardly tucked behind her ears. She was just admiring her silhouette and enjoying the warm nicotine taste on her tongue, when she heard a chuckle behind her. She spun around on her heel to find John standing less than three feet from her.

"Must you insist on sneaking up on me like that?" said Peggy with her green eyes flashing. She tipped her chin in frustration and embarrassment at having been caught in such a flagrant display of self-admiration.

His blue eyes twinkled as he smiled down at her, and she felt her heart tighten in her chest.

"Maybe if you weren't so intent on admiring yourself in the window you would have noticed that I was standing right here," said John.

"Well, I've noticed you now! What are you doing down here anyway? Isn't there some lavish event that you need to attend uptown?"

"Actually, no. I was just about to stop and get some lunch at La Signet. Since we have found each other, would you care to join me?" he offered his elbow to her.

"It's the weekend. You don't want to have lunch with me on the weekend," she demurred.

"It isn't a working lunch. We can just have lunch. As friends?" she was sure that she heard an uptick at the end of his sentence, the hopeful question. Were they friends? She supposed so. They worked closely together, and he had invited her to that grand soiree at his parents' house. He seemed to appreciate her more than anyone else that she knew, and he saw her talent for writing and journalism.

"As friends," she nodded and took his elbow.

40

The young dark-haired waitress laid their plates on the table between them. A Cobb salad for her, and a Monte Cristo sandwich for him.

"So, tell me, Peggy, how did it feel to see your name in print this morning?" he asked before cutting into his enormous sandwich.

She chewed her hardboiled egg

carefully and said honestly, "It was a

dream come true."

He nodded and asked "worth the

sacrifices?"

"Absolutely. Although, I don't sacrifice much. Sure, I have to make do with clothes that are not de rigueur, but beyond that, I am perfectly content in my life. I enjoy working with Caro and the others, and I have a cozy room at Mrs. Penske's. There is very little else that I could want."

"Is that so? You don't feel like anything is missing from your life?" he tilted his head slightly to the left and studied her face.

"No, not at all. I always knew that I would be a journalist, and I knew that that meant I would not marry or have children. It is nearly impossible for a woman to have a career and a home life. If I were to marry, I would automatically be expected to leave my job and care for my husband and my home. I could even be fired for getting married, let alone pregnant. I can't let anything derail me from my goal," she answered earnestly.

"What if the right person came along? Perhaps you would not feel so strongly about your plan," he said with a twinkle in his eye. Peggy blushed as though he had read her thoughts when they had strayed to the idea of falling in love, and with him in particular. Could he tell that she sometimes imagined the idea of them? He couldn't. She was nearly certain that she did not let those thoughts show when they appeared.

"Absolutely not," she answered with all the conviction she could muster, "That would never happen because the only right thing for me is to one day have a..."

"A what?" he asked after she trailed off.

"You'll think I'm silly, and knowing your propensity for laughing at me, you will definitely laugh," she replied haughtily.

"Scout's honour, I promise not to laugh," he said holding up two fingers.

"Well, one day... one day, I am going to have an office like yours – with a window overlooking the park, a big wooden desk with a nameplate with my name on it, and a huge, cut-glass ashtray next to my typewriter. That, and my name on the masthead. That's how I will know I have made it." She looked up at him with fervour. She could swear that he looked slightly proud of her.

He nodded and took another bite of his meal.

"You know, things are changing. It's 1966, not 1952. You don't have to give up one part of your life to have another anymore. Look at the women we cover in the Women's Pages. They are demanding equal rights and looking for ways out of the kitchen. Maybe it would be possible for you to have both... one day." She looked at him for a long time, thinking that this was not the first time someone had told her that she would regret not falling in love, but this was the first time someone had suggested that she could have it both ways. Usually, people acted like she had two heads when she shared her desire to be a journalist over a housewife. Usually, they acted as though she had said she had a plan to run away and join the circus. But not John. John suggested that maybe she could choose both. Maybe she could be the woman who went to the Important Job and the woman who fell in love. She considered what he had said and nodded once.

"It's true things are changing, but not fast enough. Look at the women in the typing pool – as soon as they fall pregnant, they are out. Evangeline was let go just last week because she had gotten married and is now expecting her first child. That won't be me."

She speared a slice of ham and popped it into her mouth, while he considered what she had said. "What about you?" she asked, "You're single and don't seem to be all that keen to let go of the bachelor lifestyle."

"Don't be so sure," he said a tad grimly.

"Don't be so sure that you are single?" she felt her heart plummet to the bottom of her stomach.

"No, don't be so sure that I am enjoying the bachelor lifestyle," he confessed, "When I see Eliza and Perry, I sometimes wish that I could find what they have. They just have a rhythm and they make each other laugh, and it just looks so... nice."

At the mention of Eliza, Peggy felt the flush of embarrassment at her long-held belief that he was engaged to her. She looked across the table at John, admiring the way the forelock of his shiny black hair fell forward on to his brow, the way his eyes shone as he spoke of the idea of falling in love, at the solid line of his jaw, and not for the first time, Peggy wondered if there was a way that she and John could make a relationship work, that would allow her to fulfill her dream.

41

May 29, 1966

Dearest Daisy,

I am writing to you from the west coast. It is beautiful here – mountains that touch down at the ocean, beautiful weather, and people working for real change. I wanted to let you know that Helen and I are settling in nicely. We found a groovy apartment that is walking distance to the beach. I've decided to sue for a divorce. Tom and I are not meant for each other, and I don't think that will ever change. It's not the same shame to be a divorcee out here as it was back in Hamilton. Here people are more free and love is more readily available. You won't believe this, but I now own bell bottomed jeans, and I have a job! I'm working at a free clinic in the city that provides healthcare to people who can't afford it. We even offer the pill to women who need it. I think you would really dig the scene out here, Daisy my darling.

How are things with you? I received the clipping of the Trib with your name printed on it. It's hanging on my fridge now so I can tell everyone that that is my baby sister. I'm so proud of you, Daze. I hope one day you might be proud of me, too. I am really building a life out here, and I hope you can come out and see it one of these days.

Anyway, got to go! Helen and I are heading to a music festival tonight to hand out pamphlets for the clinic. Write soon.

All my love and a kiss,

Lindy

Peggy smiled to herself as she folded the letter back up and tucked it into the envelope. Her straightlaced sister had used the word "groovy" and was now wandering around in bellbottoms handing out pamphlets to provide women with the pill. She would never have imagined it for Linda, but she was so glad that she was happy. She hoped that Tom wouldn't fight the divorce. She had a suspicion based on the conversations she had had with her brother and her mother that he would not want to draw attention to his current living situation, and that a quiet divorce might be the best thing for everyone.

Peggy turned to the window and lifted the sash, letting the fresh late spring air enter her room. She was glad to know that Lindy had received the clipping of her first byline and was proud that it hung on her fridge where all and sundry could see it.

She picked up her glass of iced tea and took a sip while mentally composing her reply to Lindy. She checked the back of the envelope in her hand and saw in her sister's tidy loops that she now had an address where Peggy could find her. She put the tea back on the little table next to her window seat and walked to her desk, pulling out her Filofax, and neatly printing the address into a slot below Lindy's name. She also noted that Lindy had written Linda Brennan, so Peggy copied the same into her address book.

Peggy was covering her typewriter for the night and had just tossed the paper cup of coffee into the wastepaper basket to the left of her desk when she heard footsteps approaching.

"Are you heading out?" John asked, when she turned towards the sound.

"Yep. I'm done for the day and am looking forward to Mrs. Penske's lamb shank for dinner and a nice glass of wine. What about you? Are you done for the day?"

"Not quite, but let me walk you out," he said, reaching for her light spring jacket, the last one remaining on the coat rack at this time of the night. He held it open so she could slip her arms into it, and she felt a frisson as his thumb brushed the nape of her neck.

"Oh, you don't have to do that," she protested, but he insisted, so they walked to the elevator bank and he pressed the down button. They stood together in silence waiting for the doors to open. Once inside, she asked "What are you working on tonight that has you burning the midnight oil?"

"Budgets. We aren't getting enough advertisers for the Women's Pages as I would have hoped. Some of our old advertisers aren't happy with the new direction that we have taken things. They were much more comfortable when we wrote about Bella Healy's wedding dress, or 9 new ways to use Boullion cubes," he said with an air of frustration. She knew that it really mattered to him that the pages represent the modern woman and that women were more interested in politics and equal pay than they were about Bundt cakes.

She gently laid her hand on his shoulder, "you're doing the right thing," she said. He looked down at her and gazed into her eyes. Peggy swallowed and stared back at him. He placed his hand over hers and for a moment she thought he might lean in and kiss her, and she was sure that she would reciprocate if he did.

The doors of the elevator suddenly opened, and the spell was broken, Peggy quickly withdrew her hand and blushed. Of course he wasn't going to kiss her, he was her editor and they had been talking about budgets for crying out loud. She quickly exited the elevator and began to rush to the broad glass doors at the front of the lobby when she heard him call to her.

"Peggy?"

She stopped and turned on her heel to

look back at him, blushing at her

foolishness. "Yes?"

"Thank you." The elevator doors closed again and he was gone.

She turned back to the glass doors and pushed her way out to the darkening street and rushed towards the station to catch the last train heading back towards home.

"Girls! You will never believe what happened at the shop today!" Rita was extolling loudly at the dinner table. Peggy was daydreaming about the moment in the elevator with John and was not paying particular attention to what Rita was saying as she cut into the rich, gamey lamb shank in front of her.

"I was busy stylin' a mannequin in the front window when the grooviest fella walked into the shop. He came around and told me that he was in the market for a shag jacket, like the kind Sonny wears, and as luck would have it, we had just received some of the shaggiest shag jackets that you ever did see, so I helped him find one that fit like a glove. Next thing ya know we were just jawing away, and he says he's got two tickets to see Gordon Lightfoot at the Centre tomorrow night, and he asked if I'd like to join him! Seriously! Me!" Peggy barely heard what was being said and was startled when Em nudged her.

"Sorry, what?" she asked looking from Em to Rita.

"I was sayin' I'm goin' to a concert, and I need ya to help me choose my outfit. I need to look my best, ya know?"

"Oh, sure, Rita. I would be happy to. Although, you know a lot more about fashion than I do," Peggy said, observing Rita's bright purple and green ensemble.

"This ain't just about fashion! This is a date, and I wanna look like Sharon Tate, ya know?" This made Peggy smile, because Rita and Sharon Tate bore not even a passing similarity. It was like asking an apple to dress up as an orange. But Peggy smiled and nodded, "Sure, Rita, I'd love to help you. Let's take a look at your closet after dinner."

Peggy reached for her wine glass and took a sip, enjoying the sour flavour, which paired so nicely with the succulent lamb. She still could not get it out of her mind that John might have kissed her had the doors not opened when they did. She felt sure that there had been a moment of electricity between them. But she knew she had to be crazy because he was her boss. There is no way he thought of her in the way that she sometimes thought of him. She was determined to let this silliness go and to focus on her work. She thought back to her mother pressing her father's shirts and starching their collars and sat up a bit straighter, newly resolved to not let frivolous notions keep her from what she was working so hard to become.

She looked around the table at each of the young women that she was so lucky to call friends and housemates and thought how each of them was on their own path to becoming what they wanted to be. She knew that marriage was in the cards for many of them, but she just did not see that for herself. Look at Caro – she was a successful journalist, had a life of her own, and did not rely on any man to take care of her. That was what she wanted.

After dinner, Peggy and Rita ascended the stairs to Rita's room. As always, there were clothes everywhere. Hanging out of the closet, piled on the chair, thrown over the bed and in messy piles on the floor. Clearly, Rita had been hunting for something to wear before work that morning... or a tornado had entered the house and Rita's room was the only one affected. Peggy shoved a few miniskirts, and a pair of dungarees to the side and sat down cross legged on the bed, facing the closet.

"Ok, Rita, what have you got in mind?"

43

The sky was bright and warm. A perfect early summer day. Peggy walked from the train station to The Tribune building, inhaling the fresh air deeply. She was excited to see what the day would bring, and what article she was to be assigned, because she was confident that after what she deemed the success of her recent article, she knew that she was going to be writing more and getting further ahead, each week. It didn't occur to her to worry about what John had said about the advertisers being unhappy with the direction of the women's pages. She was too busy imagining what it would be like to be nominated for a Pulitzer Prize.

She pulled open the heavy glass door and entered the lobby, her neat black pumps clacking on the tiled flooring. When she reached the elevator, she was reminded of her ride with John the night before and couldn't help but blush at the memory. She rode the elevator to her floor and was approaching her little desk when she noticed some Important Men entering John's office. She wondered what that was about, then hung her hat and light summer jacket on the coat rack and set down at her desk. She had been planning to ask John if he had anything interesting for her to work on, but as he was otherwise occupied, she set about typing up her notes from the recent interview on which she had shadowed Caro. She could hear muffled voices from John's office, through the transom, and even though the men spoke in hushed tones, there was an air of seriousness that piqued Peggy's curiosity.

After what seemed like an age, the Important Men opened the door and filed out of John's office. Once they had rounded the corner of the corridor, Peggy stood, and smoothing her black corduroy skirt, she walked to the doorway of the office they had vacated.

"Good morning," Peggy said brightly, while simultaneously reading the room for signs of what the meeting had been about. John looked up at her from his desk and ran his fingers through his hair. He looked like he hadn't slept, he wasn't wearing his tie, and his shirt collar was open.

"Oh, morning, Peggy," he said.

"Everything ok?" though clearly everything was not okay based on his appearance, "Did you even go home last night?"

"No, I ended up working through. Everything will be fine; the powers that be are just concerned that we are not bringing in enough revenue."

"Can we fix that?" Peggy asked, leaning against the doorframe.

"Yes, but we will have to make some changes, unfortunately. We can't afford to keep running the women's pages if the advertisers stay spooked. We have to find a way to get them on board, or we will be back to running stories about cake walks and knee highs," John said, sounding a little defeated.

"But surely, they know that that isn't what women want. Surely, they know that women are more engaged with our stories than ever before!"

"Are they? I wish there was a way to prove that, so we could demonstrate to the executives and the advertisers that women are reading the new section and are happy with it."

"We will just have to find a way. What if we ran an article asking for feedback? What if we asked the readers to share their opinions on the new section and to let them show us how they feel?" Peggy asked quickly. She could not handle seeing all their hard work go to waste, and even worse, she could not bear the idea of returning to the typing pool. How long would she be stuck listening to Mr. Latham before she rose back to the level of journalist with a byline if the women's pages went back to what they had been? No, she simply had to find a way to fix this before it was too late.

"That's not a bad idea. Go grab Caro, and meet me in the boardroom, we need to figure out a plan," said John, as he began to gather papers from his desk.

Peggy pushed off the doorframe and turned to head

to Caro's office. She began to think through her plan, and to figure out how to make it a reality, so that they could continue to expand the women's section, rather than have it return to its old formula. She wished that the advertisers were women, because then they would know what women were interested in. Women did not just care about dish soap and vacuum cleaners. They were more than mothers and wives. They had goals and interests, just like men did. Women cared about the war in Vietnam. Women cared about the next Prime Minister. They wanted to know what Lester B. Pearson was doing. They were interested in art and music and books. They needed more than cake recipes and how to clean a diaper by bleaching it in the sun. She knew this because she was women. She wanted to know these things, and that was the job of a newspaper! To provide news. It should not be up to advertisers to decide what was printed.

She found Caro editing a story she had written in her office. She hurriedly explained what was happening and the two women made their way to the boardroom, where John was laying out papers on the table.

"Okay," he said, sounding slightly more upbeat than he had in his office minutes ago, "we need to find a way to get advertisers back on our side, so we can see some revenue, without, as Peggy astutely put it, letting the advertisers dictate which stories we cover. Peggy suggested that we write an article that asks women to provide us with feedback about the changes that we have been making. I think that is good, but I also think we need to re-engage our focus group."

Caro sat down in one of the chairs around the large table and pulled out her notebook. "Do we want the same women as last time, or a whole new group? The reason I ask is that they already told us what they wanted to see covered and that is what we have been doing, so maybe we need a whole new demographic of women to provide new insight into what women want," she said.

Peggy nodded in agreement, as she also took a seat and prepared to take notes.

"That's a good point, Caro. Okay, Peggy, I need you to speak to Mrs. Kelly about getting the focus group together. Caro, I need you to begin drafting the story."

Peggy felt a twinge of jealousy that the more senior of the two women was tasked with drafting the article that had been her idea, while she was sent on an errand to speak to Mrs. Kelly, but she brushed it aside, as she knew that they all needed to work together in order to solve their problem before it became a serious issue.

44

Peggy sat at her desk sifting through the letters that they had received from the story that Caro had written, and they had published in the most recent women's pages. The stack was abundant and she was doing her best to sort them into piles based on the tenor of the letter. The "I love what you have done and want to see more" letters went into one pile; the "I can't stand that you are giving into the feminists and want my recipes back" letters went into another pile; and the "I don't know what to think, but decided to write anyway" letters went into a third pile. Once sorted, Peggy intended to count each pile and see which response had been greater. She was beginning to feel a bit disheartened, though, by just looking at the stacks, because the second pile seemed to be growing faster than the first. She was wondering if it was possible that people who loved to complain were more likely to respond to a call for letters than those who were content.

John came over and pulled over a chair from a neighbouring desk.

"How is it going?" he asked pleasantly, eyeing the piles.

"Well, not too badly. It seems like we have a fair amount of people who are happy with us," she pointed to the stack to the left of her typewriter, "but we also have a fair amount of people who think we are communists."

"Communists! Really?" he chuckled as he picked up the stack of missives from the right of her typewriter. She watched as he thumbed through the letters, bemused.

"Yes, apparently by treating women like thinking humans, we are communists and are running The Tribune into the ground. They don't really have suggestions for what we should cover, but rather just have a lot of ideas about what we shouldn't," Peggy said as calmly as she could muster. She was frustrated that negative people would be so negative. She had imagined that there would be some people who didn't like the new direction, but she didn't expect to be compared to Karl Marx.

"People love to complain, Peg, and we just gave them the perfect outlet for it," he said. Once again, she noticed the way he used her pet name, and it made her heart skip a beat. He smiled over at her, and she noticed how blue his eyes were against his dark hair. "Just try not to take it personally."

Try not to take it personally? How was she supposed to do that, she wondered. These people could single-handedly take away all the advancement that she had made in the last year, by forcing her back into the typing pool if they could not convince the advertisers that what they were doing was working! How could she not take that personally?? Mrs. Timothy Johnson said that they were "pinkos" and Mrs. Arthur Sorensen wrote that they were ruining the institution of The Tribune by putting things that would traumatize the average woman into the venerable Women's section. It was personal because she cared about what they produced and she cared about what readers thought about The Tribune.

"I'll try" she replied, though she knew she'd have better luck scaling the Empire State Building than she would not taking the letters personally. "What can I help you with, Mr. Grant?"

"I was just checking in on your progress with the letters," he said, looking as though there might be more to why he had approached her desk than just that. She imagined him asking her to dinner, just the two of them and then him walking her home, and then... she stopped her thoughts before they trailed too far. They had work to do.

"Well, the letters are going as well as can be hoped. How is it going with the focus group preparations? Has Mrs. Kelly found enough willing women?"

"It's going well. I believe she had gathered 25 women, and our hope was to have 30, so we are nearly there. Now for them to represent the ideals that we are wishing for. That remains to be seen," he said, rising from the chair. "I'll leave you to it. Please let me know as soon as you have your count."

She watched as he walked back to his office and then returned to her sorting. Mrs. Harland Matthews wanted to know whether we could send her the recipe for Dutch apple pie that we had printed recently, as her copy had gone missing and her mother-in-law would be visiting and it is her favourite. Peggy heaved a great sigh and placed the letter into the third pile. Dutch apple pie, indeed!

At the end of the day, Peggy had 36 letters in favour of the change, 38 against, and 26 that had nothing to do with anything. Her heart sank as she tallied the last letter. She knew that these were only the first batch of them to come in, but she had hoped that they would fall into her favour. She was desperate for another shot at a byline, and this was her best hope. If they could not keep the advertisers happy, proving to them and the Important Men Upstairs that what they were doing was worthwhile, they would end up returning to the old style of the women's section, and she knew that there was no place for her there. Caro and Mrs. Kelly had managed quite well on their own and it was likely that they would handle it just as well if they had to. There would be less to do, and at best she would go back to being a nameless staff writer; at worst, she would be sent back to the typing pool. Then she realized that no, in fact, at worst she would lose her dream job at The Tribune because they had likely already filled her position in the stuffy, smoke-filled bullpen. She felt a burning at the back of her throat as her green eyes filled with tears. She jammed the palms of her hands into her eyes willing the tears away. She would absolutely not cry at her desk. She was Hal Brennan's daughter. Tears were for the weak. Or at very least tears were for when one was alone in one's bedroom. She would not let them see her weak.

She imagined Mr. Brennan sitting across from her and telling her "Never let them see you down. If you want to be taken seriously in this life, you can't ever let them see you struggle. Fake it, 'til you make it, Margaret. Fake it, 'til you make it." She would. She would do absolutely anything to keep on track of her dreams. She had worked so hard and done so much in the last year that she could not imagine giving it all up.

45

"Peg! The phone's for ya!" shouted Rita from the hall. Peggy crawled out of bed and opened her bedroom door. She took the receiver from Rita, and picked up the telephone, stretching the cord so she could bring it into her room. She shut the door behind her, and slumped down on to the floor, with her back against the side of her bed.

"Hello?"

"Hello, Peggy, it's Mother," said Mrs. Brennan through the miles between them.

"Hi Mom," Peggy was grateful to hear the comforting tones of her mother's voice. There was something so soothing about it, that Peggy almost cried again. She had spent the hours since dinner curled up in her bed, on the verge of tears, "how are you?"

"I'm well, thank you for asking. How are you?" Mrs. Brennan asked.

"I'm... oh, mom... I don't know how I am!" She spilled the whole story about the advertisers, and the very important men, and the letters, and being accused of communism, and everything that had happened in the last couple of weeks. She felt a tear stream down her cheek as her mother sighed. "I don't know if I can do this anymore."

"Peggy, darling, then why don't you come home? I know you wanted to be a journalist. I know that you have been living in the City on your own but look where it has gotten you. If you were at home, you could work for Daddy at the office. Of course, it wouldn't be writing, but it would be typing, and isn't that almost the same thing anyway? It would be so nice for Joanie and I to have you nearby to help with the little ones." Her mother sounded almost hopeful as she spoke. Peggy could picture the softness in her mother's grey-green eyes as she spoke. They had had this conversation so many times, but this was the first time in a while. The first time since her mother had come to help her make the dress.

"Mother, you know I can't do that. I love you, and Joan, and the kids, but I need to do this for myself. I need to prove that having my name in the byline was not a one off. I need to prove that I can do this."

"Honey, who do you need to prove it to? No one expects this off you."

"Myself, mama. I need to prove it to myself. I can't let go of my dream because of a bump in the road. I want to be a writer. A journalist. Someone who asks the questions and gets to the bottom of things." She realised as she spoke that she meant it. She could and she would do this. It was just a bump in the road. She was determined, and she knew she was talented.

"Well, then, I guess you just answered your own question, darling. Just remember that you always have a choice. You can always come home, and you can always be strong. You just have to decide what you want to do."

"Thank you, Mother. I don't know how you do it, but you always know just what to say to help me through," Peggy leaned her head back against the comforter and wiped the tear from her face. She took a deep breath, and knew in her heart of hearts that she was where she needed to be. She was doing what she needed to be doing and she would succeed. She and John and Caro would produce impactful news and fill the women's pages with things that mattered like the fight for equal pay, and the right to not lose a job because a woman marries. Sure, they would also include the recipe for Mrs. Campbell's carrot cake, and run stories about the latest society event, but they would also run news. They would not let a bunch of Phyllis Schlafly doppelgängers stop them. They just had to find the way.

"Margaret, have you heard from Linda lately?" Mrs. Brennan was asking.

"I received a letter a couple of weeks ago. She seemed in good spirits, and wrote that she was settling in out west."

"I just heard from Tom that she has sued for divorce. Of course, Tom is absolutely devastated," said Mrs. Brennan. Peggy sucked in her breath. She didn't know how much her mother knew about Tom's roommate, and she did not want to risk exposing him. If what Harry said was true, then he could face serious consequences.

"Divorce must be hard. I am sure Linda didn't come to this decision lightly. And at least there aren't any children. They can both start over. Besides, Linda is our priority, not Tom, and Lindy is happy. She is working at a clinic with her friend Helen, and she said they are living close to the beach. It all sounds pretty great from where I'm standing, Mom."

Mrs. Brennan sighed. Peggy pictured her sitting at her little telephone table in the hall, tapping out her cigarette in the little pink ashtray next to the phone. Based on the time, her hair was likely already in curlers, and she was wearing her old faded pink house dress.

"You're right, Margaret. I just worry, and no Brennan has ever gotten a divorce, so it makes me so sad that Linda is to be the first. All I have ever wanted was for you children to be happy, so it breaks my heart when any of you aren't."

"I don't think Lindy is unhappy now. I think if she were to continue to be married to Tom she would be but living her own life out west is good for her."

"I suppose," said Mrs. Brennan, before changing the subject to George's oldest daughter Eloise's ballet

recital. Peggy closed her eyes and listened to her
mother speak in italics about how absolutely lovely
Eloise and her friends had been on stage.

46

She sat next to a large, sweaty man and tried her best to lean away from him but found herself being bumped every time someone walked down the aisle to enter or exit the train. She bit her lip in frustration and counted the minutes until she reached her stop. Peggy was not patient by nature, and summer weather on the train was stretching what she did have very thin. When her stop arrived, she clamoured off the train as quickly as her espadrilles would allow.

When she arrived at the office, she stopped for a paper cup of the hot, tarrish coffee, regardless of the heat. She knew that she needed her morning cup of coffee to start the day and today was to be a big day. Today was the second focus group, and she would be observing while John and Caro ran the group. It was her job to pay attention to body language and make notes of who seemed keen and who seemed to be frustrated or angry about the changes. She rushed with her coffee to her desk and burned her lip as she took a quick sip in motion.

"Darn!" she cursed and then glanced around to see if anyone had heard. Luckily, she seemed to be on her own. She continued to her desk and set the paper cup on the corner and turned to see if John was in yet. His door was open, so she went over to say good morning.

"Hey there, kid", he said as she entered his office, "ready for today?" He indicated that she should sit in one of the two chairs across from him. She chose the left one and smoothed her yellow dress as she sat. He looked especially handsome this morning, dressed in a light summer suit, with a blue tie that matched his eyes almost exactly and his hair Brylcreemed back from his face.

"Yep, ready as I'll ever be," she said brightly. She had dressed for the occasion, in a bright yellow smocked sundress with a light, white cardigan and her raffia espadrilles tied pertly at her ankle. She was sure that the ensemble complemented her auburn hair and her dusting of freckles just so. She wanted the people in the room to be impressed by her, and she wanted John to see her looking her best.

"Good. We've got about an hour before our guests arrive, so go ahead and get started on the article about Hans Larson's house. We will head down to the seminar room in about 45 minutes."

"Alright, will do."

45 minutes later, she was deep in thought when she felt a hand on her shoulder; she looked up and there was John.

"Time to go," he said. Her shoulder felt warm

where his hand had been and she had to remind
herself for the millionth time that John was her
boss. She could not be distracted by her attraction
to him, because she had to admit to herself at least,
that she was attracted to him, today. Or any day for
that matter! She silently nodded and picked up her
Filofax and a couple of pens and rose to follow
him.

They entered the seminar room on the second
floor, where chairs had been arranged in a
classroom style, to accommodate the 30 expect
people. Peggy found a seat near the back of the
room and placed her Filofax on the table in front of
her, and uncapped her pen, as Caro ushered the
guests into the room.

"Please, help yourself to refreshments, and take a
seat wherever you would like," Caro said, with her
brightest Pan-Am smile. Women and men began to
shuffle in and made their way to the coffee carafes
and muffin platters under the window. Peggy
thought briefly of the coffee she had forgotten on
the corner of her desk, and sighed. It would be a
long day without her coffee. She contemplated
joining the queue, but she didn't want to risk spilling
coffee while she was busy taking notes.

Peggy looked around the room and found herself
imagining what each of the participants would be
like. There was a woman with frizzy hair, not unlike
her own, carefully picking the blueberries out of her
muffin and popping them into her mouth one by

one. There was a man wearing grease-stained overalls under a sports coat. There was another woman who was carefully pouring coffee into a cup with hands that shook so badly the carafe set to rattling. There was a woman who was impeccably dressed in a smart purple suit, with a jaunty hat seated in the first row, gloved hands folded neatly in front of her.

Would they help to save the women's pages, and her journalistic career or would they dash her hopes faster than the letter writers had?

"Welcome," said Caro over the din of people settling into seats and introducing themselves to their tablemates. Peggy counted it a blessing that no one joined her table, so she could examine the guests in peace.

People began to settle and quieted down, so John and Caro walked to the front of the room.

"Welcome," Caro said again, as she smiled at the people gathered in the room, "thank you all for coming today. We appreciate your willingness to talk to us and to help us with the direction of our women's section here at The Tribune. I'd like to introduce our editor, Mr. John Grant, and I am Caro Nance, a reporter here at the paper."

"As Miss Nance said – thank you for coming. We are looking forward to hearing your opinions and your suggestions," said John, with a charming smile.

"I assure you, sir, you do not want my opinion,"

interjected a man in a polo shirt and khaki pants, near the middle of the room. Peggy looked towards him, with his glowering face.

"We do, even if it unfavourable to the paper as it exists today. We want to ensure that our readers are well informed and enjoy reading the stories that we run," John said, without skipping a beat. Off to a rocky start, but John and Caro began their questions, and Peggy took notes. Some of the opinions were in favour of the new changes, some were vehemently opposed and some were undecided. The blueberry woman felt that the changes were not drastic enough and wished to see the women's pages abolished, as she felt that it was infantilizing to have a separate section in the newspaper for women, when women could clearly read the rest of the paper as they wished. Peggy was actually in agreement with this, but she still wanted the section, as she knew it would take her far longer to get her next byline if she was thrown into the deep end, up against the longstanding journalists that the paper was known for.

The meeting had been going on for over an hour when a man who had been sitting quietly near the back, a row in front of Peggy suddenly announced that he would be cancelling his lifelong subscription to The Tribune if the women's section did not go back to covering "womanly things". When pressed, he said that his wife needed to know how to defrost the deep freeze, not to know how many Americans had been killed in Vietnam. He said she had looked forward to the women's section once a week, and since the change he couldn't bear to hand over the section. Peggy bit her lip to keep from speaking out. She felt her cheeks go red at the idea that this man felt he could withhold the newspaper from his wife in case she learned what was going on in the world. It was so infuriating that Peggy wanted to give this man, in fact, she wanted to give a good percentage of the people in this meeting a piece of her mind. She hated the idea of women being treated as inferior. She hated men and women who felt that they had the right to dictate what another person could know. Her innate curiosity was what had led her to the field of journalism, and she knew there were more women like her. Mr. I-want-my-wife-to-defrost-the-freezer, Miss. I'd-rather-see-dress-patterns... well, then they could do those things without telling other readers what they could and could not have access to.

47

Peggy stood next to her desk in the darkened office while Mrs. Kelly gathered her bag and her things to head home. It had been a long day, and it was not yet over for Peggy, Caro and John. They wanted to complete their analysis of the focus group before the executives met in the morning. They wanted to prove their case for keeping the women's section as it was, and for their plan to convince advertisers to come back.

"What say you, ladies? Shall we order in Chinese?" John suggested, knowing that they were not going to be going home any time soon. Peggy and Caro agreed. Peggy could almost taste the tangy pink glop that that they coated the sweet and sour pork in, she was so hungry. She noticed that Caro was now walking around in her stockinged feet, shoes abandoned in her office. Peggy admired Caro's ability to be at home wherever she was, whether in a dark and empty office, a flashy dinner party, or interviewing politicians. Peggy wondered if she would ever be like that; she hoped so. Peggy wondered if she dared take off her cardigan, now that nearly everyone was gone. She was so hot that her frizz was sticking out at all angles and she would love to just take the little sweater off and toss it on the back of her chair, so she could focus on their work rather than on how incredibly warm she was.

She looked at Caro and decided that she would take the sweater off if it was her, so she did. She was just hanging it on the back of her desk chair when John came in with the menu for the Chinese takeout restaurant. She looked up and noticed him taking in her bare shoulders and hoped he would not be offended and make her put the clammy cardigan back on. But he didn't seem to be looking at her in an offended way, he seemed to be looking at her in a way that she couldn't quite put her finger on. Caro looked back and forth between John and Peggy and lifted one perfectly arched brow and smirked.

"Shall we order?" she asked, reaching for the menu.

"What? Um... oh... yes, let's order. We have a lot to do and it is already 7 o'clock," said John, shaking his head slight and turning his attention to Caro.

Once the food arrived, John removed his tie and loosened the top two collar buttons of his shirt and joined the women who were sitting at the boardroom table with the tiny white cardboard boxes spread around them. No one stood on ceremony and each grabbed a carton and some bamboo chopsticks and dug in.

"So, what did you think? Do you think this will help or hinder our cause tomorrow?" Caro asked John, as he shoveled a mouthful of chow mein noodles into his mouth.

John chewed thoughtfully and said, "I think it will

help because we have the opinions of our readers, which should help us to convince the executives that we know what we are talking about."

Peggy devoured her carton of sweet and sour pork as they mused on what information had been the most valuable and what they could discard. She thought she caught John looking at her with the same look he had worn when she had removed her cardigan throughout their dinner, but when she caught his eye, he would simply give a small smile and continue eating.

After they finished their supper, Peggy gathered the empty cartons and carried them to the trash in the kitchenette next to the typing pool. She checked the pot, and decided to make more coffee, as she knew that the three of them would need something to keep them awake through the night. She was just pouring three cups when she felt someone approach from behind her; assuming it was the janitor, she carried on with what she was doing.

"Can I help?" asked John, coming to stand next to her.

"What have I said about sneaking up behind me?" said Peggy with a start. He chuckled as he reached for one of the coffee cups. His fingers brushed her hand as he took it and for a moment, she thought her skin was electrified, she looked up at him, pink rising in her cheeks. John looked down at her and bit his bottom lip in a way that made Peggy want to reach up and kiss him. They stood there for a long moment, neither moving, their fingers still touching.

Peggy took a step towards John and they were mere inches apart. John inclined his head ever so slightly towards Peggy, and as Peggy tilted her head back, she suddenly found herself wanting to kiss him more than she had ever wanted anything in her life. More than moving to the city, more than working at The Tribune, more than anything. He stepped forward and closed the distance that remained between the two of them and just as his lips brushed hers, they heard Caro approaching and jumped apart, as though they had been burned.

"There you are! I was starting to think the rats had all abandoned ship and left me to figure this out on my own," Caro said as she briskly entered the kitchenette, "Ah! Coffee! Lifesavers, you are!" Caro stepped between them and grasped a cup.

"Come on then," said Caro, swiftly, unaware of what had happened just moments before she entered the room.

They worked through the night, analyzing the information, and compiling the letters, but through it all Peggy could not stop thinking of the moment that John's lips had brushed hers. It did not quite qualify as a kiss, but her lips burned as though it had been. She couldn't help but wonder what it had meant. Did this mean that John thought of Peggy in the same way she thought of him? She wanted to ask him, but there was no time. They had to prepare John's presentation for the executives, and she certainly could not bring it up with Caro in the room. That didn't stop her from absently touching her lips, as though she could still feel John's.

Around 3 o'clock in the morning, they finally finished their work, and Caro offered to give Peggy a ride home, as there were no trains running at this time of the night. Peggy gladly accepted, as the idea of walking all the way home at this time of the night did not appeal to her, and she desperately needed some sleep before she returned to work at 9 o'clock. They drove mostly in silence, but when they arrived at Peggy's boarding house, Caro surprised her by saying:

"Be careful, Peggy. If you really want to be taken seriously as a journalist, you don't want to give the impression that you are willing to date the boss to get ahead."

Peggy was dumbstruck and quietly thanked Caro for the ride, as she exited the vehicle and made her way to the front door, pulling out her keys as she walked. How had Caro known? Surely, she couldn't have seen them in the kitchenette. Was she that obvious in her admiration of John? She didn't think so, but maybe she was. She felt her anxiety rise as she let herself into the house. She did not want to be seen as dating her way to the top. It was so unfair how women were treated – firstly, she was expected to be content as a secretary, then she was supposed to get married and quit her menial job, to have babies and keep house, or if she decided to be a career woman she was faced with every barrier under the sun, and she had to worry about how she was perceived by others, because she could be accused of not earning what she had worked so hard for. It wasn't an even playing field for women.

She entered her room, shut the door and opened the window, as the little attic bedroom had become stuffy from the heat of the day. She changed into her nightgown, dropping her clothes and leaving them where they fell. She was spent, physically and emotionally. She crawled into bed, peeling off the comforter, and curling up under just the thin sheet. She thought about the moment with John, and then what Caro had said. She fell into an exhausted sleep shortly after her head hit the pillow.

49

Peggy awoke slowly, the thin light between the curtains slicing through her room and hitting her face just so. Her head was pounding and she felt as though she needed at least three more days of sleep. She looked at the clock on her bedside table and saw that it was 8 AM. She still had an hour to get to work, thank goodness. There would be no time for Mrs. Penske's delicious breakfast, but at least she would make it before the executive meeting. She felt anxious as she dressed and brushed her hair. She could already feel the heat of the day entering her room, so she knew that it would be another scorching hot day. She left her window open but closed the blinds to keep the sunlight from turning her bedroom into an oven.

She hurried down the stairs, and waving to her friends, she rushed to the train station. She still felt exhausted. The late night had worn her out. She just hoped that they would receive good news today, and that they would be able to convince the executives to get the advertisers back onside. She needed this to work because she really, really wanted her work to be noticed and she really, really wanted her byline to be more than a one-time thing.

She rode the train, tapping her foot impatiently the whole way. She noticed a man looking at her with frustration, but she could not bring herself to stop, so she gave him what she considered to be a conspiratorial smile and carried on tapping.

When she arrived at the newspaper, she rode the elevator, sighing in agitation each time the doors opened ahead of her floor. When she finally reached her floor, she rushed to her desk, trying not to remember the night before, and to just focus on this morning. She didn't want to think about the moment when John and she had nearly kissed; she didn't want to think about what Caro had said when dropping her off. She just wanted to focus on getting through the day and getting the advertisers on their side. She noticed that John was not in his office, so she peeked into Caro's office, and she was not in there either. A glance at her watch told her that it was a little after 9, so John was probably already in the meeting. She did not know where Caro was, but she was a little relieved not to have to see her first thing this morning. She did not want to rehash that moment in the car, and she did not want Caro to judge her for not having said anything before leaving last night.

Peggy typed up an article, half-heartedly. She kept one eye on the entrance to the corridor, and one eye on her work for most of the morning. How long could it possibly take to share their findings? How long could it possibly take for the Very Important Men to make their decision? She felt like she was on tenterhooks as she both wanted the news and was worried that the decision would not go in their favour. Caro returned to the office shortly after 10 o'clock, having been at an interview for an upcoming feature. She did not say anything to Peggy about the night before. In fact, she seemed her usual cheerful self and asked only if John had emerged from the meeting. Peggy felt relieved to avoid an awkward conversation and told her no, that John had not yet emerged. She said he had already gone up before Peggy had arrived that morning, so she did not have any information at all. Caro went to her office to begin typing up her notes, and Peggy returned to her work. Around noon, Peggy decided to go down to the cafeteria to find some lunch, but as she was leaving her desk, she saw John approaching and all thoughts of hunger evaporated. She had to know what had been decided; food could wait.

"How did it go?" she asked urgently.

John smiled at her wanly, the lack of sleep and stress visible on his face.

"It went. They are discussing now how to convince the advertisers that we are doing what the readers want. If they can convince the advertisers, then we can keep running our section the way that we have been, but if not, we are to go back to the old way of doing things. They used the words 'subversive' and 'radical' to describe what we have done, and I don't think they meant it in a good way."

Caro, upon hearing John's voice, emerged from her

office to hear what was being said. She leaned against her doorframe with her arms crossed across her chest and listened.

"So now we wait," John said, looking as though this was the last thing he wanted to do.

"Do we continue with the articles that we had planned for this week?" Peggy asked, "Or do we have to wait to find out what sort of section we are running first?"

"Keep doing what you are doing now. We won't know for a while, and we still need to get this week's pages out."

Peggy nodded and returned to her typewriter, not wanting to linger longer than necessary. Not with Caro standing in the doorway, watching like a hawk. John walked to his office, and Caro returned to her typing.

"Peggy, can you come in here for a moment?" John said quietly. She followed him into the office, and he shut the door behind her. She sat down in one of the chairs across from his desk, and he went around and sat in his chair. She thought that even as tired as he was, he still looked shockingly handsome.

"About last night," he started, and her heart sank. She did not want to have the 'about last night' conversation. She was sure he would say that it was a mistake and that he regretted it, and she did not want to hear that. She wished she was back at her desk. She wished she were anywhere but here in this moment.

"I'm sorry," he said, "I should not have kissed you. It was deeply unprofessional and I am so sorry. I have been thinking of it all night and..." he trailed off, as Peggy lifted her chin and looked at him imperiously.

"Not at all, Mr. Grant," she said in what she hoped was her iciest tone, "I am also to blame. It won't happen again. Now, if there is nothing else, I should get back to writing that article, if we have any hope of publishing it on Sunday."

She stood up quickly, and turned on her heel heading for the door, hoping he did not see the redness in her face, or the tears prickling her eyes.

The word came down two days later. The executives had managed to convince some of the advertisers to give the new pages a shot. Three major advertisers had decided to pull their ads, but most had decided to stay. It would take some budgetary finagling, but they would be able to keep their section and continue to produce the news that they wanted to report on. Peggy was so relieved when she heard the news that she absented herself to the ladies' room, to have a little cry in peace. Her article would appear on Sunday. She would have her second byline, after all.
Now if only she and John could work together

without any awkwardness, she would be completely happy. They had barely spoken, outside of expressly work-related issues since that morning in his office, where he apologized. It hadn't even been a kiss. Their lips had barely touched, but he had regretted it, and she would not give him the satisfaction of seeing her hurt. If he could carry on as though nothing had happened, then so could she. She could and would be as professional as possible.

50

Peggy returned home at the end of the day and after helping herself to a cup of tea in the kitchen, she climbed the stairs to her room. She set the teacup on the little table next to her window seat and settled in, digging through the cushions for her current notebook. She found it and a pen and began to write.

This time not story ideas but rather her feelings. It had been a long time since Peggy had written anything so personal, but she thought of that night with John and poured her heart on to the page. She allowed herself to feel her disappointment at his reaction. She wrote of wishing that he had not apologized and rather had wanted to kiss her again. To kiss her fully and properly. She wrote of her fear that they would not be able to continue the women's section, and about the relief that they would be able to continue it the way that they wanted to. She wrote of her frustration that the three major advertisers had pulled out. She wrote of the disappointment and challenges of being a woman in the newspaper industry. She wondered if there was anywhere, other than being a homemaker that a woman could get ahead. She wondered why it was ok for men to fall in love with colleagues, and no one thought anything of it, but if a woman fell in love at the office, she was trying to use her feminine wiles to get ahead. She wrote about the unfairness of a man choosing to marry and being allowed to continue working, but if a woman did, it reflected poorly on her. She wrote about everything that had been causing her anguish over the last few months and allowed herself to be angry, and sad, and frustrated.

She allowed herself to cry in the solace of her own tiny room, knowing that no one was there to judge her or make her feel weak. After she had finished writing, and had finished her tea, she sat back against the cushions next to the window and fanned her face. It was still stiflingly hot in the attic bedroom, even with the window having been left open all day. She looked at the clear blue sky, through the tree out front and thought how nice a day of rain would be. She glanced at the clock next to her bed and saw that it was dinner time. She did not feel like joining the girls at the dinner table, but she was famished. She did not have the energy to hear about Rita's dating life, now that she had found Rufus, and she did not want to explain her tear splotched face. She just wanted somewhere cool, and quiet to eat. She checked her purse and saw that she had two dollars, so she changed into a fresh sundress, and her espadrilles, washed her face and snuck down the stairs, so as not to draw attention to herself.

She walked along the sidewalk until she reached the small diner on the corner of the next block, and feeling that familiar monster in her belly, she pulled the doors open and stepped into the air-conditioned space. She felt her hot skin cool instantly. She found a table near the window and began perusing the menu, quickly deciding on a hot turkey sandwich and a glass of iced tea. She lit a cigarette as she waited for the waiter to come take her order and felt the immediate sense of calm that the smoke provided her, as it hit the back of her throat. Once she had placed her order, she sat back and observed the patrons, as was her wont. She glanced out the window and saw people passing and wondered what their days had been like. She wondered if they also felt as melancholy as she did in this moment. And then she saw him. John was walking past the window, in his dungarees and a polo shirt, unbuttoned at the collar. She attempted to duck her head so he would not notice her, but all she managed to do was knock over her glass of iced tea and spill it across the table. The waiter rushed over with a rag and began mopping up the spill, as Peggy apologized profusely, trying to sop up some of the spill with her napkin. When she looked up again, John was no longer out the window, he was standing next to her table, with an amused smile.

"Were you hiding from me?" he asked once the waiter walked away.

"No!" she said with a tilt of her pointed chin, trying to look as haughty as she could manage with an iced tea stain on her dress. John slid into the chair across from her and tilted his head in amusement.

"I think you were. As soon as I saw you, you tried to duck your head and ended up knocking over your glass. Why would you hide from me?" he asked with a hint of a laugh in his voice.

"I was not hiding from you. I was... the sun hit my eye, and I went to shield my face, and..." she stammered.

"Peg," he said quietly, "what's going on?" he looked at her with kindness in his blue eyes.

"Mr. Grant," she started, then noticed the slight wince at the formal address, "John," she began again, "I don't know what you mean. There is nothing going on. We are colleagues... you are my boss, and I think we both need to remember that. If I recall, it was you yourself who said that what happened between us was deeply unprofessional and should never have happened. I am simply respecting your wishes and trying to keep things between us professional. You and I want the same things – I want to get ahead in my career, you want to have a successful Women's Section, we both want what's best for The Tribune."

"We can be professional at the office and still speak to each other outside of the office; it's not a one or the other situation. If I could take back that moment in the kitchen, I would, but I can't so I was doing what I thought was best for you," he said.

"What was best for me? What was best for me? You don't get to decide what is best for me! I am an adult and can make my own decisions. If I want to kiss someone, it's my choice. I am so tired of people thinking that they can make my decisions for me or telling me what to do. If I don't want to kiss someone, then I won't. I don't need to be treated like a child."

"I don't want to take advantage of you, Peggy. I like you, more than I should, and I am your editor. I don't want people to get the wrong idea about your success. You are a truly talented writer, and will make a fine journalist, but not if people think that you 'slept your way to the top'."

"For Pete's sake, you sound just like Caro! I know I don't want people to have that impression of me, but I have worked so hard to get where I am..."

"And I don't want to take that away from you," John interrupted.

"...and I have never imagined finding space for love in my life. But with you, I can imagine having it both ways – having a successful career, and maybe love, to," she finished, as though he had not interjected. She instantly felt like she had said too much. She hadn't meant to tell him how she felt about him, or how she imagined being able to have love and her byline with him. The embarrassment rose on her face and she covered it with her hands.

"Peggy," he said quietly, and she suddenly did not

want to be here any longer. She needed to leave and retreat to her bedroom. She could not believe she had allowed herself to be so vulnerable and to share her feelings with John of all people. She quickly opened her little handbag, dug around for the two

dollars, dropped it on the table and stood up.

"I have to go," she said hurriedly, "I need to... I need to... not be here." She didn't allow him time to reply and rushed from the diner as quickly as she could, her knees shaking as she walked, or rather bolted down the street. How could she have been so foolish? She should never have told him. Her temper got her every time. She should never have shared her feelings with him. How were they going to work together after this? She had just blown any chance she had of getting ahead. John would never treat her like a colleague again after this. She continued walking at a ridiculous pace, and uttering to herself. She did not take a moment to consider whether she looked like a crazy person, she just kept going. She passed her boarding house, before noticing and doubling back. She rushed up the stairs and nearly knocked Rita over in the process.

"Peggy Sue, what on earth is going on? Why are ya in such a rush?" Rita exclaimed, before noticing Peggy's face. "Peg? What's wrong?"

Peggy looked at her friend and felt the sharp sting of tears in the back of her throat. She stopped in her tracks and collapsed down on to the front steps,

Rita slowly taking a seat next to her, and taking her hands in hers.

"Oh Rita, I have really made a mess of things," said Peggy. She told Rita everything, from the moment in the kitchenette, all the way through to what had just happened at the diner. She poured out her heart and told Rita how devastated she was, and how she knew she had just moved further away from her goal, rather than closer to it. For the first time in her life, she had allowed her heart and not her head to lead and now she was certainly doomed.

"Oh Peg, ya aren't doomed. I'm sure that John will not hold this against you, ya know. And from the sounds of it, he was just as involved in that kiss..."

"Almost kiss," interrupted Peggy.

"...alright, almost kiss as you were. And ya never gave the guy a chance to say his piece tonight, ya know? He mighta told ya that he was just as head over heels for you as you are for him. Ya never know, because you ran out on him so fast," said Rita, with her usual candor. Peggy sniffled through her tears and wiped them away with the back of her hand, smudging her makeup in the process. She looked up to the sky that was a long way from turning pink with sunset and tried to catch her breath. The heat of the day had not lessened, and rivulets of sweat travelled down the back of her neck.

"Rita, you don't understand – he told me he regretted it and apologized for it even happening. There is no way that he feels the same as I do," said Peggy.

If only she had stayed on track with her goals, this never would have happened. Why had she ever begun to think about love at all. She should have stayed focused. She began to regret having met John, but at the same time knew that his direction for the new Women's Pages had helped her immensely in her rapid career advancement. She knew that she was a talented writer, and would have earned her byline, but through working with John, she knew that she had arrived there faster than if she had simply been in the typing pool reporting to Mr. Latham.

"Peggy, listen ta me, he probably felt like he needed to apologise because he didn't know how you would react. Maybe he feels just as anxious about all of this as you do. Maybe he would have told ya today if ya'd given him the chance, ya know?"

Peggy tried to steady her breathing and to compose herself, holding on to Rita's hand as though it was an anchor keeping her moored. Was Rita right? What would John have said had she stayed? Was it possible that he did not regret their moment together? Was it possible that he also wanted more from their relationship?

"Do you think that's possible?" asked Peggy through

her sniffles.

"Of course it's possible," said Rita, pulling her friend in for a hug. Peggy embraced her tightly, enjoying the comfort of the hug. She began to regain control of her breathing and slowly her sobs came to an end. She wondered what John would have said, if she had given him the opportunity to speak.

"Peggy Sue," said Rita quietly.

"What?" asked Peggy letting go of her embrace and looking at her friend.

"There is a man coming who looks like he is looking for someone," she nodded down the street towards a handsome dark-haired man who did indeed look like he was looking for someone. She realized with a start that it was John. He must have tried to follow her. She imagined that her face must be red and blotchy from tears, and she did not want him to see her like this, but she also did not have the energy to run away for the second time in one day.

"Oh, my goodness," said Peggy, "that's him; that's John."

"Really?" said Rita with great

interest, shading her eyes to get a

better look at him.

"Don't stare!" said Peggy

exasperatedly.

"You need to talk to him. Now's as good a time as any," said Rita, getting up and brushing herself off. She leaned down to kiss Peggy on the cheek and then continued down the steps to the street.

51

"Hey, Peg. Mind if I sit down?" John said when he reached her stoop. Peggy indicated for him to sit in the spot that Rita has recently vacated. He sat down, with his hands on his knees and looked at her. His forelock had fallen on to his brow, and he had beads of sweat along his forehead. "You left in a bit of a hurry, so I didn't get a chance to tell you how I feel," he said quietly.

"How you feel?" Peggy repeated, looking into his face searchingly.

"Yeah," he said, "Peggy, from the first moment that I saw you trying to catch snowflakes on your tongue, I have been head over heels for you. You are the smartest, funniest, strongest woman I have ever met and if I could, I would spend every moment with you. I love working with you, but I also just love you."

"You love me? But why did you say it was a mistake and wouldn't happen again, then?" Peggy asked confused.

"Because I am your editor, and I didn't want anything to come between us, and I was afraid that you would have regretted it, since you have said so often that you do not have space for love in your life. I was... I was afraid, Peg," he finished quietly. Peggy did not know what to say, so she did the only thing that made sense to her in that moment. She took his hand in hers and brought it to her lips. He slid his hand from hers and gently reached for the back of her neck. They leaned in closer and soon their lips met. Peggy sighed at the feel of his warm lips against hers. She searched his lips with her tongue, until it found purchase. The kiss was sweet and exactly as delicious as Peggy had imagined it would be. She brought her hand up to caress his cheek, as they kissed. His warm hand cupped the back of her head, and she felt like she was immersed in nothing but this moment. Their lips parted and the looked into each other's eyes, each searching for something.

"John," began Peggy, but she did not know what to say. She did not want to spoil this perfect moment by saying the wrong thing. She wondered if he felt the same way. The way he was looking at her gave her the feeling that he was.

She licked her lips, as though she could still taste his mouth on hers, and he leaned in for another kiss. This one was more frantic, more searching than the first. Peggy allowed herself to fall deeply into the kiss, matching his energy with her own. She forgot that they were sitting on her front stoop and that anyone could come by and see them, she did not care in the least. Her mind was filled with only thoughts of John and this kiss. She wished it would go on forever.

52

On Monday morning, Peggy dressed for work carefully – she chose a sundress with cap sleeves and a full skirt, and her nude pumps. She thought the overall effect was darling, and secretly hoped that John would feel that way, too. When she arrived at the paper, she found a small gift wrapped on her desk, in front of her typewriter. She looked around to see who had placed it there, but no one seemed to be around. She looked at the tag – "to Margaret Anne Brennan". It was certainly meant for her, as she was the only Margaret Anne Brennan in the building. She removed the ribbon and unfastened the paper.

Inside was a simple brown box, but when she lifted the lid, she found the most beautiful cut glass ashtray she had ever seen. In the centre of the ashtray was an engraved **MAB** in an elegant font. It was the ashtray of her dreams, the one she would have on her desk when she had her own office.

"You said your goal was to have a cut glass ashtray and your own byline," said John, leaning on his office doorframe, arms folded across his chest, "and since you have already earned your byline, I figured you might be in the market for an ashtray."

She ran her fingers over the engraving and looked up at him with a broad smile, her freckles dancing across her nose. She put the ashtray down on her desk and walked over to where John stood, and standing on her tip toes, she kissed his shaven cheek.

"Thank you," she murmured, "I love it. Now I just need to earn my own office, and all my dreams will have come true!" she silently added "and then some" as she knew that she had never imagined that she could have all this and John. John was a new addition to her dreams, but now she could not imagine them without him. They would make it work, their careers and their relationship. John knew that Peggy was ambitious and had no intention of giving up her career to remain at home as anyone's wife, and he would have her no other way.

THE END